Horace Gordon Hutchinson

Creatures of Circumstance

Vol. III

Horace Gordon Hutchinson

Creatures of Circumstance
Vol. III

ISBN/EAN: 9783337053031

Printed in Europe, USA, Canada, Australia, Japan

Cover: Foto ©Andreas Hilbeck / pixelio.de

More available books at **www.hansebooks.com**

CREATURES OF CIRCUMSTANCE

A Novel

BY

HORACE G. HUTCHINSON

AUTHOR OF

"GOLF" (BADMINTON LIBRARY), "FAMOUS GOLF-LINKS," ETC.

IN THREE VOLUMES

VOL. III.

LONDON

LONGMANS, GREEN, & CO.

AND NEW YORK: 15 EAST 16th STREET

1891

CONTENTS OF VOL. III.

CHAPTER   PAGE

I.   FATHER AND SON SQUARE ACCOUNTS .   1

II.   THE LAST AND BEST OF MRS.
ETHEREDGE.   13

III.   COLONEL BURSCOUGH'S BEST TONIC .   29

IV.   SYBIL AND ROBERT   45

V.   A COVERT SHOOT   68

VI.   THE HOUSE PARTY   86

VII.   STORM WARNINGS AT WHITE-CROSS
ABBEY   103

VIII.   FILIAL INGRATITUDE   126

IX.   DEEP WATERS   145

X.   MR. CHEADLE'S EXILE   173

XI.   DOUBTS AND DIFFICULTIES   185

XII.   HUSBAND AND WIFE   199

CHAPTER   PAGE

XIII. "The Woman that deliberates"   219

XIV. A Terrible Mistake   235

XV. "In the Evening there shall be Light"   256

XVI. The Nemesis of Weakness   266

CREATURES OF CIRCUMSTANCE.

CHAPTER I.

FATHER AND SON SQUARE ACCOUNTS.

MR. CHEADLE, senior, paid but flying visits to Pebblecombe. One evening, in his little parlour, he was meditatively discussing a pipe, and "Fishy schemes," of sorts, when there came a tapping at his parlour door, and, following the tapping, the tapper in the person of Mr. Cheadle, junior.

"Well?" the young man said tentatively, as if to sample the parental mood.

The sample that turned up was the

ironical. "Well, got tired of your diggings ? Think you'll find it cheaper to live on your poor old father than to pay your own way—eh ? Got cleaned out ? I only wonder how you've lasted so long. I haven't given you any money since you came here, have I ? "

Young Cheadle absolved his parent of any such misdirection of capital.

"You've been a terrible expense to me one way or another, what with your excellent and religious education, your clothing, your food. Merciful heavens, how a boy eats !" said Mr. Cheadle, in pious admiration.

"Well, governor," young Cheadle answered ; "I've been a heavy expense to you, I guess. That's so. Well, look here. You just make out your account, d'you see, of how much you've spent on me—since the very day I was born if you like. You just tottle it all up the way it should be. Don't spare anything. Put it all in. Then I'll just write you a cheque for the whole lot, and then we'll be quits, once and for all; and I'll have done hearing for ever this lamentation of desolation of yours over all the money I've cost. Put in the interest, you know. Cal'clate it all up at four per cent. from the start; and I'll give you a cheque for the lot."

"You'll do what?" old Cheadle asked, almost gasping with astonishment.

"I say I'll write you a cheque for the lot."

"Psha!" said Cheadle. "Gammon! you haven't got the money."

"Oh, I reckon I'll have credit enough to pay you what you've spent on me. You can wire to Coutts' whether my cheque for two thousand of your pounds will be honoured."

"Two thousand pounds! You! Two thousand pounds lying idle at Coutts'. Why don't you invest it—invest it in—in the Metropolitan Fish Consumers' Association? Write me a cheque for it, my dear boy—and I'll invest it for you. My son — I've only just learnt your worth!"

"Guess that's so, governor," young Cheadle assented; "but I've learnt your worth long ago. Thanks—I think I'll manage my dollars myself — good old man!"

Now, that is just where Mr. Cheadle

was not a good business man. He was too emotional. His son's balance at the bank had fairly upset him from his own balance for the time. He really did love his son in that one moment with a fervent, generous love, such as one great artist may feel towards another. His son's answer acted liked a shower bath. He saw his mistake, and at once withdrew into his colourless, ironical mood. "And where, may I ask, did you steal it?"

"Well," said young Cheadle, in his deepest nasal—a triumph in one who had so little of the organ left—"I did not steal it from my own friends, or from gentlemen whom I had led to consider me as their friend. I did not steal it by promoting some darned fishy Company, and trying to get all my friends, and even my own son,

to subscribe to it.   No matter to you how
I got my money.   I did not get it that
way."

Mr. Cheadle looked like one sorely
grieved.   For a moment he seemed too
pained to speak.   Then he said, with
effort—

"And this from you—from you whom
I but now called my son! whom I have
brought into the world, fed, clothed,
educated, sent to America," said Mr.
Cheadle, as though this last were the
crowning blessing.   "Would to heaven
you had stayed there!   As it is, I disown
you—go!"

Mr. Cheadle made a majestic gesture,
showing his son the door.

Young Cheadle, with his hands in his
pockets, sauntered towards it.

" When will you have that account made out, governor—for my maintenance, and so forth ? To-morrow ? "

"Go !" his father repeated, with still greater majesty.

Young Cheadle took one hand from his pocket, and opened the door.

" Stay !" said his father, with a note of trouble in his imperative.

Young Cheadle leant, half in and half out of the room, against the door post.

" You said four per cent.," observed his father. " The usual rate of interest on arrears is five."

" All right," said young Cheadle, " make it five."

He shut the door, and left his father to his meditations.

" God bless my soul," ejaculated Mr.

Cheadle, senior, as the door closed, "and can that be my son ? I have been a fool," he continued. "That boy might have been my right hand, if I had but led him aright. That boy has coolness, which is a better thing than cleverness ; and he may be clever too. He might have helped me greatly. As it is," croaked Mr. Cheadle, like a gloomy prophet of lamentations, "he is going to be a millstone about my neck, an adder in my path. Anyway," he concluded briskly, "he shall pay his maintenance bill, and I hope he'll like the look of it. The more I charge him, the better father I shall appear. It is beautiful both ways."

Till a late hour Mr. Cheadle was busied on the document.

When complete it ran thus :

	£.	s.	d.
To Nurse £2 2s. a week for 1 month	8	8	o
To Doctor for Mrs. C——	20	o	o
To Doctor (whooping cough, measles, &c.)	15	o	o
To clothing—			
(a) long clothes (complete outfit)	15	o	o
(b) short clothes	7	10	o
(c) knickerbockers (two sailor suits per annum for 5 years at 9s. 6d. each)	4	15	o
(d) trousers (2 suits a year for 9 years at £2 10s. each) ...	45	o	o
To shoes, hats, hosiery, &c., for 15 years	60	o	o
To maintenance from o to 19 at 1s. per diem = £18 5s. per annum ...	346	15	o
To schooling (books, stationery, &c., with extras, at £60 per annum, for 6 years)	360	o	o
To pocket-money and sundries—say	50	o	o
To houseroom (rent, rates, and taxes free, use of china, linen, plate, &c.)—say	100	o	o
To value of American property—say	500	o	o
	1532	8	o
Interest at 5 per cent.—say ...	500	o	o
	2032	8	o

" P.S.—Mr. Cheadle, senior, begs to say that in consideration of the extreme difficulty of determining the exact amount, in each case, of the items, he has studied to place them rather below than above the actual figure. Further, he will be content to waive all claim to the odd pounds and shillings, and will give a receipt for the whole in return for a cheque for £2000."

"To Nurse!" said young Cheadle next day, as his father handed him the document. "Hum—you seem to have begun at the beginning."

"I did my best to do it conscientiously," said Mr. Cheadle, in the sad way in which we speak of a painful act of duty.

"Hum—don't remember having the whooping-cough," the son remarked, as he read.

"Naturally," replied the father. "You took the affliction young."

"Hum—s'pose that's so. By-the-bye, I didn't know I was nineteen when I went

to America.   Still, that's a point you
should know best."

He made no further observation about
the account, but the broadening smile
which rippled on his features as he read
interfered with the melody of " the Braes
o' Mar."   The humour of the situation
was not wasted.

The amount of the sum total he scarcely
glanced at, but kept looking from his father
to the account, and back at the account
from his father, as if he were engaged in
a physiognomic study, trying to trace the
connection between the two.   His father
gazed sadly out of window, with the expression of one whose griefs are heavy
upon him.   Then young Cheadle pulled
out his cheque-book, and wrote and signed
a cheque.   He handed it to his father,

saying, " There, governor, that squares us then."

Mr. Cheadle examined the cheque carefully. He exclaimed in soliloquy, " By Jove ! " Then he folded the cheque carefully and put it in his pocket. As he did so, he said with a sigh, " Well, all I can say is I hope it has been honestly come by."

Young Cheadle did not answer. And in this way father and son squared accounts.

CHAPTER II.

A QUEER thing happened. Mrs. Etheredge sent for Lady Morningham.

Sybil was in her own little writing-room when the note came. This room was dearer to her perhaps than anything on earth. It was an ever sympathising friend, and in all her introspections she saw herself there in her favourite seat. The room was furnished with oak. The fireplace had an ingle nook like an old cottage fireplace. It had dogs for log faggots, which were heaped beside the ingle nook in an

(13)

old oaken thing that had once been a child's cradle. But where Sybil loved to be was in the window-seat. It was like a square box. On either side was a seat for one, so that when two sat in the window they faced each other. A slight oak pillar stood from the ground to the roof of the box at the inner corner of either seat, and above ran a rod hung with a curtain, which could be drawn so as to make this little recess a room apart. The windows were square and latticed. Who has seen the window-place of Mozart's room at Salzburg? That is it.

Happiness for Sybil—such happiness her life now gave her—was to sit in the gown that she loved best, which was always of a fashion and colour to harmonize with the little cottage room, in this window-seat. Here she watched the rooks every evening hurrying up from the seaward joys of Pebblecombe and Little Pipkin, and assembling in their multitudes to croak their evening hymn of praise before settling down upon the trees. In this, woman is certainly feline—in her love of place, of one room, of one seat— and she grows so the more in lack of the opportunity for the nobler canine affection towards the beloved master.

Sybil was in the seat, and in the mood and dress, that she loved best when the servant came with Mrs. Etheredge's note. She took it carelessly enough from the salver, looked puzzled as she began to read it, frowned as she turned quickly to the end to see the signature, then turned back again and glanced hastily through it. " I won't go," she said decidedly.

Then she read it again. "'Beg you to come to me," she read, muttering to herself. "'Low fever—am dying.' I don't believe that. 'Assure you my own peace of mind, and yours no less, depend on your granting this my last request.' What can she mean ?"

Sybil's eye wandered thoughtfully over the dear room, over the gorgeous symbolical and sacred pictures, with their wealth of warm colouring lighting the dark oak. In one of the cabinets was hid away a pile of pictures of quite a different sort—Robert Burscough's— pictures that he had given her before he had proved false and broken—no, not that, but turned her heart to stone. That was how these pictures stood in her mental catalogue. She seldom looked at them now. Generally, when she did so, she brought them out with a sigh, and after studying them awhile, put them back with something much like a curse. But now she went to the cabinet and looked them over once more.

Sybil had her full share of the failing which Satan took advantage of so soon. " Yes," she said to herself, as she replaced the pictures, and once more glanced at Mrs. Etheredge's letter, " I will go ; it is my duty."

Human motives are complex. Sybil might have some foundation for calling it " duty." But certainly the " duty " part of it began to be forgotten and overwhelmed in a very strong tide of

C

curiosity as the time for the visit came nearer.

When she was ushered into Mrs. Etheredge's bedroom, one glance at the face which looked out at her, with wan, hollow eyes, from the pillow, assured her that Mrs. Etheredge had said no more than truth when she described herself as dying. For many years she had enjoyed the immunities of the *malade imaginaire.* She had been wont to refer to her constitutional delicacy in terms so pathetic as to make her hearers involuntarily speak to her in hushed tones. Her malady had defied diagnosis, for its chief symptom was a general inability to perform the most obvious duties if they were at all distasteful. It is a form of incapacity often found with the minor poetical temperament.

But the enjoyment of even the most delicate health can preserve no one indefinitely. Mrs. Etheredge caught a form of low fever which has since become notorious under the misnomer of " Russian influenza." She nursed herself carefully, and soon got the better of it, which is a perilous thing to do. Russian influenza is seldom dangerous, because the sufferers feel too wretched to do anything but stay in bed and be sorry for themselves. But convalescence is dangerous, because the convalescent is anxious to get up and run risks.

In course of getting better Mrs. Etheredge caught a chill, and things began to look critical. She talked much of her plans for the winter, and then things could not have looked worse. While in perfect health, she had declined discussion of any

future project in a few pathetically murmured words, which suggested the idea
that she was unlikely to live to see its
fulfilment. That she should be really ill,
and be speaking of her future plans,
augured badly. That she should strive
to thrust away the prospect of death
showed that she was afraid. A few days
later the doctors told her that there was
no longer hope, and she sent for Lady
Morningham.

Never, since her childhood, had Mrs.
Etheredge been so good and true a
woman as when she lay on her deathbed.
She was a good woman, at the last, because
she was a simple and a natural woman,
though she was bowed down morally by
the load of many past follies. There was
a dignity in her reception of Sybil which

she had never achieved in the days of her affectations.

"It was good of you to come, Lady Morningham," Mrs. Etheredge said. "Forgive my having to receive you in this room, in this way. I once did you a great wrong. I want to put it right—at least, no—not that—that is impossible, unhappily. But I want to confess it to you, and so put it in such train that some day perhaps it may come right."

Sybil did not trust her overmuch, even on her deathbed. She looked at her to read her meaning, but the weary eyes looked back in utter indifference of her scrutiny with the serene gaze of one for whom the mundane future is nothing. It was Sybil's eyes that fell, but not before they had learned that in her perfect freedom from all earthly hopes and fears it was unlikely that the dying woman would tell her anything but truth.

And, after all, what was it that she had to tell—this confession which the circumstance of approaching death seemed to envelope in such a tragic atmosphere? It was a very little thing indeed. It was that once in her drawing-room in London, when she knew Sybil was intending to call, she had endeavoured to lead on Sybil's lover to make a declaration of love to herself. She told the unlovely tale with all the cynicism of despair.

She had failed to elicit from him such a declaration. "I knew," Mrs. Etheredge said, "that even if he did tell me he was in love with me, it would not be true. He was a boy, and did not know his own heart, but I knew it better than he did. I knew that he loved you, with every bit of the true feeling of his nature, though for the time being I had caught and bewildered his imagination. You see," Mrs. Etheredge added, with her first touch of human, feminine emotion, " you see, you had the advantage over me of knowing him longer (though you do not seem to have really known him), and you had the advantage of me in years (as you once reminded me)."

Sybil hung her head, in hot shame.

" No matter, Lady Morningham. I deserved it—all that, and far more ; but I do wish that you had not dealt me that taunt about my age—it was cleverly done too, I remember it all so well—if only for your own sake. If you had not done that

I do not think I could have behaved so abominably to you. Now I tell you this," she went on, with more strength in her voice, raising herself on one elbow in the bed, and looking straight into Sybil's eyes— "Even if Robert Burscough had made me the most passionate avowal of love in all the world, you ought to have known him better than to have believed it. You ought to have known him better than he knew himself, if you loved him. You ought to have known that he was but a boy, whose head could be turned—but not his heart—by any tolerably good-looking woman who cared to do it. I had tolerably good looks, and he liked them. Yes, he liked them," she said, aloud again, "but there it ended. And that very day that you came to call upon me, he was telling me that he liked them, that I was first among his friends, that I gave him back sympathy for sympathy—but—— Yes, there was a 'but.' At that 'but' I stopped him, for you had come into the room a moment before. I knew what was to have followed that ' but,' though it seems that you were not able to supply it—'but,' he was going to say, 'the entire love of my whole life is given for Sybil Davies.' That is what he was going to say. But I stopped him, because I hated you. Oh, God, forgive me," she said, sinking off her elbow and pressing her face upon the pillow, " God forgive me for all my mean-ness and my malice, and God forgive you too, Lady Morningham, for all your wilfulness."

Sybil scarcely knew what she was doing.

She knelt down at Mrs. Etheredge's bed-side, and without any thought about the form of her prayer, prayed for God's help. Her mind was in a fearful tumult, as she dimly recognized the life's blessings that misunderstanding and her own haste and the malice of the dying woman on the bed before her had combined to put out of her reach ; but, over all the tumult, the master-note that rang clear was one of triumph— " Robert had been true to her—true. He had not swerved in his allegiance one hair's breadth ;" and in this thought her heart was exultant.

When she rose from her knees, Mrs. Etheredge said feebly, " I fear I must ask you to go. I have tired myself too much. I have no more to tell you. Good-bye," and she held out a wasted hand.

But after a moment's pause, Sybil shook her head. "No," she said, "forgive me, Mrs. Etheredge, but I should be acting a lie if I were to take your hand now. I could not do it honestly."

"Very well," the other answered indifferently. "Good-bye."

That night Sybil woke after a short sleep. Her heart felt very tender, as she thought of Robert; but her conscience tortured her so sharply that it was all she could do to refrain from getting up, then and there, with some wild notion of going to Pebblecombe to see Mrs. Etheredge, to beg her forgiveness, to take her hand. The counsels of sanity prevailed, and she decided to go the first thing in the morning.

But in the morning Mrs. Etheredge

was beyond the reach of human hand-
shaking, for she had given back to her
Maker the life which she had caricatured,
perhaps more than most, by her transparent
affectations.

CHAPTER III.

COLONEL BURSCOUGH was much affected by Mrs. Etheredge's death. He had admired her immensely, and his pity for her as a deeply wronged woman went perilously near to love. He was regaining his strength, and in resuming his cheroots had resumed his position of the oracle of the Little Pipkin cricket ground, with Mr. Slocombe as his devoted henchman. It seemed wonderful to Robert how little things had changed in his absence. He had been moving quickly, and was con-

(29)

scious of many changes in himself. Little
Pipkin had been standing still, and neither
Mr. Slocombe nor the parrot seemed to
have another grey hair or feather between
them. They had changed less than the
shepherdesses on the mantelpiece, for
many of them had lost an arm—less than
the picture of the Arethusa on the wall,
for Robert found, with disgust, that to
his more sophisticated eyes it had grown
unlovely. The parrot still said, "Sybil
and Robert" in a way that stirred bitter
thoughts of what might have been. The
horse-chesnut tree seemed to have lost
no branches, to have put out no fresh
ones. A new tenant was in the Creature's
cottage, but that was getting on in the
direction of Pebblecombe; and otherwise
things seemed exactly as he had left them.

Mr. Slocombe, with the retentive memory of those who have little to remember, narrated to Robert the details of Sybil's visit to the cottage. When he told him how she had silenced the parrot, Robert sighed, and grew thoughtful. He had not seen her, and purposely avoided White-Cross. He knew it to be probable that he would see her soon in the social life to which a political career would introduce him, but he did not care to hurry on the meeting, nor could he form an idea of the terms on which they were likely to find themselves. At present, he was fully occupied in addressing free and enlightened electors, and for the rest devoted himself to his uncle.

Shortly after Robert's return, Colonel Burscough received a bit of news that did

more to set him up than all his tonics.
Some mysterious person, whose name he
had never heard of, made him an offer for
all his shares in the Fish Company at par.

The Colonel had been so excited that
he had walked all the way to Pebblecombe, on purpose to tell the members
of the club about this extraordinary thing.
He was received with acclamation, for
it was his first appearance since his illness.
Then he revealed the secret of his obvious
excitement, but affected to make light of
it, declaring he believed it to be a "plant."

"A plant—a jammed plant, sir—that is
—you'll see," he asserted.

"Don't you accept it, Colonel," said
young Cheadle nasally, from the depths
of an arm-chair wherein he was reclining
in great comfort, with one leg over its arm.

The Colonel did not like young Cheadle, partly because he was his father's son, and partly because his manner had a Western freedom which strikes the citizen of the Old World as aggressive.

Burscough turned on the speaker volcanically, "You sir? Who asked your advice upon the matter? I tell you that I certainly shall accept this offer, and your jammed unsolicited advice only confirms me in my purpose. There, sir!"

"Don't you accept it, Colonel—it's a plant, a jammed plant—that's what it is," young Cheadle repeated, unabashed—and his lips vibrated in faint suggestions of " the Braes o' Mar."

The Colonel moved away in wrath too great to be coherent. " Insufferable young Yankee man, that," he muttered. "Really," he added, turning to the honorary secretary (presumably in virtue of his official position), "really I think it's somebody's duty to see that young Yankee man destroyed."

But, as it proved, it was no "plant"—the Colonel did not refuse the offer. Mr. Davies arranged the business details for him through the medium of a sound little City solicitor, named Mr. Peabody—acting for the mysterious transferee. The explanation of it all, Colonel Burscough did not greatly bother himself to inquire; he was more than satisfied by the wonderful recovery of his £8000.

But shortly after the end of the legal Long Vacation, matters occurred in connection with the Fish Company which seemed to require a great deal of expla-

nation.   The thrilling news reached them
that their nice quiet gentlemanly friend
Captain Conynghame was in prison !
The good Slybacon was a felon, a convict !
It was nothing to do with the Fish Company that had brought him into durance
vile, but some fishier business still.
His name was not Conynghame at all,
nor Slybacon ; nor did anyone (possibly
not even Slybacon himself) know precisely
what it was—he had, at different times,
borne so many !

They had all liked the Slybacon man,
his manner was so pleasant, and beyond
all manner of doubt so gentlemanly.
Still, they might perhaps have borne his
loss, even in such a painful way, with
fortitude ; but how about his petition for
winding up the Company ?

A Pebblecombe gentleman, connected with the legal profession, who held a small stake in the Association, went up to London in quest of information. He did not come back empty.

The petition had been up for hearing, but as none of the legal formalities had been complied with, the Judge had no option but to dismiss it.

"Well?"

"Well, another petition has been filed."

"Really—who by?"

The gentleman connected with the legal profession turned to young Cheadle, who was in his usual posture in an arm-chair, studying an article in *Punch*.

"May I say?" the legal gentleman asked.

"Say—you can say anything you like—

it's a free country, ain't it—more or less?"

"He's filed the petition then," nodding to the graceless figure in the armchair.

There was a solemn hush for a moment.

"But — but," some one stammered, "have you any shares in this Company?"

"A few," young Cheadle said indifferently. "Say, this *Punch* of yours is no brave fat. The New York *Puck's* worth two of it."

"He's got £8000 of shares in it," said the legal gentleman in the reverential tone in which it is becoming to mention such a sum.

"Then you—then it was you that—that took over Colonel Burscough's shares?"

"Was it?"

"You say so."

"Well, warn't it ? "

" No, I took over mine from a man—
I forget his name—think it was Jones."

" The very name of the man to whom
Colonel Burscough sold his."

" Humph ; is it an uncommon name for
a Britisher—Jones ? "

" Well no—not very, certainly ; but at
what price did you buy these shares ? "

" There's some likes mutton," young
Cheadle answered, like an oracle, " others
prefers swine. You mind your business,
and I'll derned well mind mine."

" Oh, I beg your pardon. You don't,
I suppose, by any chance happen to be
thinking of wanting to buy any more
shares do you ? "

" No thanks—much obliged all the
same. Say, I'll tell you what I do want

though " — all his hearers came round eagerly—" I want to read the paper— See ? "

There had been great perturbation in the tents of the Semites, when they heard of the filing of the new petition for the liquidation of their promising Company. In the first place, they had by no means intended the Slybacon petition to die so premature a death.   It had been their policy to drag it on, as a safeguard against the filing of a petition of a serious character.   But their plans herein had been overset by the sad calamity which temporarily withdrew from a grieving world the light of Captain Conynghame's countenance.   They had not been ready with an immediate substitute for the Slybacon petition.   They had not anticipated that a *bonâ fide* one would be filed so soon; but, above all, when they found out the name of the new petitioner, they were very angry Semitic gentlemen indeed.

For just at the crisis, as it turned out, Mr. Cheadle had been taking a little, well-earned holiday. He had not spent it at Pebblecombe, for obvious reasons; but we may hope that he was spending it with pleasure and profit. It was the last moment at which a crisis was to be expected, for things had scarcely settled down after the summer holidays. So the Semitic gentlemen discussed the petition in Mr. Cheadle's absence.

A petition for the winding up of a Company sometimes means nasty things for the board; for it means that, if it is granted, all their doings will be subjected

to searching scrutiny by professional ac-
countants, and reported to the Court of
Chancery.   And if their doings do not
pass muster pretty well, the judge of the
Chancery Court may order criminal proceedings against the people who have
been naughty.

At first the Semitic gentlemen were
very wild with Mr. Cheadle, for it was
the name of Cheadle—clearly, they in-
ferred, some relative of their late managing
director—that appeared upon the petition.

Mr. Cheadle had lately resigned his
post of managing director, because, as he
said, he did not wish his name to be
too prominently brought forward.   The
Semitic gentlemen had acquiesced in this
with reluctant admiration, not so much of
Mr. Cheadle's modesty, as of his foresight

in being unwilling to allow his name to become an occasion of distrust to an ingenuous public, whose confidence he might wish to invite on some future day. Mr. Cheadle had, nevertheless, continued to hold the driving reins, though from the back seat.

For the first moment, the Semitic gentlemen deemed that Mr. Cheadle had deserted them, and, for occult reasons of his own, had turned against them. The chairman said, with a solemnity of high moral tone which was almost apostolic—

"Cheadle with all his great qualities was always, I feared, a man whom it was dangerous to trust."

Then more enlightened conjectures illuminated the gloom of the Semitic counsels. "It was doubtless all a scheme of Cheadle's to block a petition from outside." With this solacing thought, they comforted themselves, and wired for Mr. Cheadle.

But when Mr. Cheadle arrived, his wrath was so fearful that, despite all his known histrionic power, not a Semite could suspect him of dissimulation. He knew in a moment the moving hand in this petition business. He knew, and he was afraid. With fearful emphasis he denounced before the assembled Semites this petitioner as his own, his only, his erring, his misguided son.

The Semites almost wept with him as he recounted the load of benefits which he had heaped on that son's ungrateful head —the care and culture he had bestowed upon him (not referring to the cheque drawn by his son on that account), the magnificent estate in America which he had given him (without mention of the doubtful nature of the title deeds, or of the fact that, when he had accepted them as payment of a bad debt, he would greatly have preferred a ten-pound note).

Oh no! he told the Semites; there was no question of the business nature of the petition. There was no one he would not have chosen as an enemy rather than his own son. They must fight this petition tooth and nail.

CHAPTER IV.

SYBIL AND ROBERT.

OUT of the numbness to which Sybil had broken herself during the first year of her marriage, by the help of the usual narcotics of society entertainments and small triumphs, her first awakening to feeling had come in the pride and joy of young motherhood over her baby. And so she had lived on, more conscious than before of the misery of the life-fetters she had forged for herself, but still able to endure them in silence. Then came the knowledge, learned from Mrs. Etheredge on

(45)

her death-bed, that in heart Robert had always been true to her. After the first song of triumph which for a while filled her being, this knowledge brought little satisfaction, but a fever of restlessness and insubordination. Happiness had been so very near her grasp. She might so easily have had the life companionship of the man who shared her heart. Instead, she had—this! and it was her own wilful folly that was to blame! Thus she tortured herself, and to add to her torture, came this further thought that the man into whose keeping her heart was given must think her worldly, a coronet hunter, shallow, fickle—as shallow and fickle in feeling as she had once deemed him. She beat herself against the bars of her cage impotently, and could no longer stifle in her breast her passionate cry for freedom.

In her quickened feeling—though it was but quickened to the sting of misery—she began again, as of old, to seek her friend, Mrs. Athelstane. For while she was wrapping herself in her cloak of indifference and worldly cynicism, she had seen little of her. She rather dreaded this friend, with the sweet, large nature and serene, clear-sighted eyes. Their serenity was a reproach to her. But now she came back to them again, as if she sought a rest and a cooling of her fever in their depths. Mrs. Athelstane asked no question, made no complaint, only received again with joy the friend whom circumstances—if one may speak so of subjective influences —had withdrawn from her. Nor did

Sybil make any confession in set terms, though to the clear vision of the serene eyes she may have confessed much.

But her husband was pleased with her. He found in her just what he had wanted —a social queen whose throne he shared, who was worthy of the prerogatives of his title, his wealth, his intellect.   To him she was as cold as a statue, but he did not ask warmth ; and the statue was beautiful. To others she was not statuesque ; but by the vivacity of her moods, and the quickness of her sympathy and wit, could keep them at their best.   It was no effort.   She loved to draw out the best that was in each of her acquaintance, men or women, and knew how to make them all happy with a turn of her favour or attention, like a skilful conjurer spinning plates.   She loved, in the manner of the psychical sportswoman, to lay their characters bare for her inspection. If a heart or two were broken in the process, what matter? The sooner hearts were broken and done with, so much the better for their owners. Such was the creed of her despair.

The real torture of her life was the being bound to this man whom she hated. At the first, when she had been able to respect him, a certain sentiment of admiration blended with her repulsion—a sentiment which was of a nature not entirely remote from the complex thing, love.

But her husband's life had changed; and when she knew that he was untrue to her, that he had become not merely cold, but coldly vicious—an exampl f vice in its most unlovely form—her respect gave way to loathing which had no admixture of any feeling but terror. Could she go on bearing it? she sometimes asked herself, with scalding tears, in the silence of the night; and she knew that, but for her child's sake, she would more than once have yielded to the temptation of seeking eternal oblivion in an overdose of the chloral to which she resorted perforce for the temporary oblivion of some hours' sleep. But since her visit to Mrs. Etheredge's death-bed, life held in prospect one bright moment in the future—a brightness by which she was fascinated, and which yet she feared—the moment of her meeting with Robert Burscough.

He had been triumphantly elected for their part of the county. She had read

his name, and his speeches, in the local
papers. But though she looked forward
so intensely to the moment of seeing him,
she had not striven to hasten it. She and
her husband went to London for the
session, and the great moment was still
to come. Robert, too, had taken rooms
in town, and was living in the Albany
Courtyard. He still kept his studio in
the debateable region, but had done no
painting since his return. He forbore to
call on the Morninghams ; but soon found
himself launched into the social life of
London, and at length, at an evening
party, the meeting occurred. After all
Sybil's feverish expectations, it was feebly
conventional. They exchanged a few
commonplace words. She hoped he had
liked America, and congratulated him on

his return to Parliament. He answered
simply and briefly. Then some one else
claimed her attention, and when she turned
again he was gone.

Sybil felt the chill of the disappointment; but, after all, she asked herself,
what had she to expect? He must think
of her as the woman who had won his
heart to throw it away—as false, shallow,
worldly, unworthy. The simple politeness
of his manner was perfect. He might
well have treated her with an affectation of
conventional hauteur—have shown that he
felt her to have used him ill. She would
even have preferred it so. Anything
would have been better than indifference.

In the course of the next six weeks
they occasionally met thus. Then came
Christmas, and Lord and Lady Morning-

ham went to Whitecross Abbey to endeavour as best they might to enjoy its
festivities. Guests came and went, and
Sybil's time was filled with social duties.
Lord Morningham invited the visitors
himself, or bade her write to them, with
little reference to her wishes ; and to the
majority of the guests she was indifferent.
But she played her part perfectly in their
reception, and if any suspected the passion
that was raging beneath the surface manner
that to her husband was so chilling, to her
guests so sympathetic and brilliant, Lord
Morningham certainly was the last to
do so.

On a clear winter evening early in the
new year, as the sun was sinking in
crimson, frosty splendour behind the hog's
back of the Downs, Sybil came cantering

on her beautiful Arab up one of the grassed avenues to the great door of White-Cross Abbey. As she came to the gravel sweep before the house, she pulled up.

"There, do you see, my Sheik?" she said, turning to the sunset and patting her pet on his glossy, golden neck. "That is where we have been—right up there on the hog's back, where that red-faced old sun is resting to wish us good-night. Didn't we have a glorious gallop, you splendid Sheik? You love it, don't you, just as much as I? It is miles better than the Row, isn't it? And what a good, brave fellow you are to carry me along so, and make me forget all about myself and the world, and the bad, wicked woman I am! Oh, Sheik darling, if it were not for you and for baby, I think it would have to be—chloral!"

She bent down and kissed his neck, and he gave a little snort of pleasure, as if he appreciated the caress, and assented to all she said.

Then she walked him up to the door, and, dismounting, gave him over to the groom, who had been curiously watching the little pantomine, and gathering the skirts of her habit, went into the house.

She had had most of the day to herself. Some guests had gone away in the morning, and others were expected; but they could hardly have arrived yet. To-morrow they were to shoot partridges, and the following day the coverts near the house. Sybil did not know who were coming. It was chiefly a bachelor party; but among

the guests would be notably a Mrs. Welbeck, a lady whom Mr. Davies would
have described as "too golden." Mr.
Welbeck would accompany his wife; but
he was perfectly broken to "down charge,"
or "go to heel" at the golden lady's command. He was generally spoken of as
Mrs. Welbeck's husband. Mrs. Welbeck
had lately become generally spoken of as
" Lord Morningham's friend."

" Mrs. Welbeck is coming," Lord Morningham had said to Sybil.

"And Mr. Welbeck, I suppose?" she
had asked quietly.

Lord Morningham had glanced at his
wife's face before answering. Then he
had said—

"Yes, certainly—of course—he is coming
to shoot, and she accompanies him."

" I understand."

Then Lord Morningham had telegraphed to Mrs. Welbeck, " Bring husband, too; say I want him to shoot."

So the Welbecks were coming, and two other men with their spouses, and three bachelors, whose names even Sybil had not thought of asking.

She strolled into the drawing-room in the dusk of the winter's evening. The lamps were not lit, and, coming in from the red sunset, it seemed darker than it was. She stood at the window, and looked out dreamily. A voice behind her in the room startled her.

" How do you do, Lady Morningham ? "

For a moment she thought it was a hallucination; for it was Robert Burscough's voice. She did not move, but stood thrilled with immobility. Then it repeated—

" How do you do ? "

She turned, and saw him smiling at her abstraction.

" How do you do," she said, still hardly recovered from the astonishment. "Why do you call me that, though— Lady Morningham ? Must you call me that ? " She asked it humbly, thinking that this was going to be his punishment of her—to treat her as one who had been a stranger to him. But she wondered at her own voice the while. It sounded to her like the voice of some one else, far away. She hardly knew what she was saying. Another self seemed to be talking, separate from her real self and hardly under the same control. But she knew that that other self was hungering for its answer.

"May I call you Sybil?" the answer came, quite simply. "Certainly it seems impossible to me to say anything else. Sybil then," he said, with an appreciative accent on the name.

The word recalled her to herself. Her heart leapt for joy. She was almost on the point of telling him then and there how she had misunderstood him, and imploring his forgiveness ; but her courage failed her, or her conscience forbade her—in fine she changed her mind. "Come and sit down," she said, "I am so glad to find you here. Are you staying here?"

"Yes," he answered laughing, "if you will let me. Did you not know? Morningham asked me—perhaps he forgot to tell you. But I'm afraid I shall not be able to shoot. I am very busy—one of the Cabinet has asked me to make a private report about trade with America. It is all Fleg you know, not me, the intelligence of anything I can say ; and he wants it in a hurry."

"Oh, how splendid," she said, with her ready sympathy, " I read your article, written from America about it, in one of the reviews. A lot of people said how good it was. You *are* making a start. But you do not mean to sacrifice your painting for it, do you ? Oh no, don't do that."

"Oh no," he replied with careless grammar, " the painting is *me*. The politics is not me, but Fleg. I am afraid

I am not by nature a politican. But it is interesting for the time being. Have you seen that dear old Fleg ? "

So they sat there by the firelight, countermanding the lamps till rung for, and talked of the old times at Little Pipkin, of Slocombe, and the Creature and the cricket—all by themselves in the great drawing room, in the hour at which the heart is tenderest and the imagination most sensitively alive.

And Sybil's heart was singing a song of triumph and peace and happiness, regardless of the bitterer moan that it must by and bye make in compensation ; for the triumph and the peace and the happiness are not the portion of those who have sinned against themselves, as she had sinned, until the Nemesis has

had its full hour. They were like boy
and girl again, and Robert found peace
too in talking to her of the old times;
and yet, he was more conscious than she,
the while, of their peril. But an hour
slipped away quite unheeded, and it
was a shock and a dismay to Sybil when
the august butler threw open the door,
and in a voice which suggested that he
appreciated the *inconvenance*, announced, to
the glimmering firelight, " Mr. and Mrs.
Welbeck."

Mrs. Welbeck could not have been
ushered upon a scene to please her
better. She smiled with golden archness
of meaning, as she dwelt on the delights
of chatting with a chosen friend, over
the red logs, in the dark. Then, with a
suggestion of intention, " she supposed

that Lord Morningham was not at home."

This introduction would be an interesting topic of Mrs. Welbeck's conversation for a while, whether with the guests of the party or with Lord Morningham, or for indirect and naively innocent allusion with the hostess herself. "Such an old friend as Mr. Robert Burscough—so charming!" For Mrs. Welbeck was sorely afraid of Lady Morningham; and never yet had the fates given into her hand so sharp a weapon, ready forged. She would not be guilty of such ingratitude as to neglect it.

The other guests arrived, and tea— and after some chat, they dispersed to dress. Ladies were in a minority. The men drew for the honour of taking them to dinner. Lord Morningham arranged the drawing, and to the expressed surprise of himself and Mrs. Welbeck, drew that golden lady's name. Robert and Sybil were separated by the greater length of the table, but he was observant both of Sybil's brilliant social gifts as hostess and of the virtual *tête a tête* established between Mrs. Welbeck and Lord Morningham. Meanwhile, Mr. Welbeck paid undivided attention to his dinner, like a good dog who deserves the reward of his docility.

When the gentlemen came to the drawing room, Robert amused himself by looking at the books on the table.

" Do you find any help in this ? " he asked Sybil, referring to a modern work which some called theological and some theosophical. " Its mysticism and its materialism touch each other very nearly, and after all is not that true? The mystic says 'be obedient to the highest motive of your own nature.' The materialist says 'you are the heir, through evolution, of all the ages that have gone before—accept your best inheritance from them.' There is little difference; only the mystic says it is of God, the materialist says it is of force or matter. But does the book help you ?"

" Indeed I hardly know," she replied wearily. " It looks as if I had gone very far afield in my search for truth, doesn't it ? After all, I suppose if it is to be altogether a question for the reason materialism is the only possible answer."

" Ah, but don't let us make it altogether

a question for the reason," he said eagerly;
" I think there must be something else.
Besides even to the reason materialism
is not a perfect answer, if we give any
weight to the argument from design.
Materialism makes the design so impotent."

"Yes, if you suppose any definite benevolence in the design ? "

" Do you mean that you doubt its
benevolence ? "

"Sometimes.   One cannot be always
brave, you know ; at least I cannot.   Has
life always gone so smooth that you
have never doubted it ? " she asked,
with a swift glance at him.

Something, a touch of passionate longing to help her, thrilled through his
veins ; but he answered quietly enough,
" I have never lost hope."

"And hopelessness is my normal con-
dition," she said with a hard little laugh.
"See, Morningham is making a move
for the billiard room."

CHAPTER V.

A COVERT SHOOT.

THE next day, as Lord Morningham came down to breakfast, he said, " You will come out to luncheon, won't you, Sybil? We shall lunch at Barker's cottage. And bring any of the ladies that care to come. Mrs. Welbeck said she would come."

It was scarcely a question, in the tone in which he asked it, and she merely replied by an indifferent " Yes."

There was breakfast at nine o'clock for the sportsmen; and at ten, or any later hour that might seem good to them, for

(68)

the ladies. The shooters stumped about in heavy boots, helping themselves to hot viands from silver dishes, with little spirit lamps beneath them, or to cold eatables from the sideboard. The conversation was desultory, and turned mainly on the prospects of the weather, and of the beat which they were going to shoot. It was a dense, damp, still, misty day.

"Thick fog in town, sure. Miserable weather," said a pessimist.

"Yes, it'll be a deadly thing for the patridges, though," replied the optimist.

"Is it partridges to-day, Morningham?"

"Yes, over these belts on Barker's beat. You know the ground."

"Burscough's late," observed one, presently.

"Oh, he's not coming," said Morningham. " Says he's busy cramming up some speech or reports or something."

" Clever chap ! "

" Yes ; queer chap though. Sort of genius, seems to me."

" Generally bores—geniuses are. Don't think he's that though."

" Now, come along," said Morningham, glancing at the clock. " It's about time we were off."

The ladies were rather late for their ten o'clock breakfast. Robert did not appear ; neither did Mrs. Welbeck. But about the hour at which the omnibus was to start to take the ladies to the shooting-lunch, she came down, looking very golden in a Redfern jacket, and a most becoming hat. Sybil could prevail upon but one other of the ladies to accompany them. They arrived at the keeper's cottage in the nick of time, for the gentlemen had just finished the last drive before luncheon, and were strolling up towards the house, where the loaders were already busy taking out food from great square baskets. They were soon seated round the cottage table, a cheery party, enjoying the picnic, and the absence of most of those minor miseries which generally attend such dissipations. Besides a variety of cold dishes, such as game, chicken, tongue, etc., and egg and other sandwiches, there was smoking hot Irish stew, and potatoes baked in their jackets. There was whisky, claret, and beer, with brown sherry or orange brandy to help down the mince-pies and fruit cake which followed the Irish stew.

"My word!" said Lord Masterton, a

wicked and rather vulgar old peer, smack-
ing his lips over the orange brandy,
"the partridges will look as big as eagles
after this!"

"Oh, do look at the beaters!" Mrs.
Welbeck exclaimed, as the shooting party
emerged from the cottage, and found the
men awaiting them with a contented, full-
fed patience. "Look at their flags! What
in the world are they for? To frighten
the birds?"

"Yes, that's it," said Lord Masterton.
"It's just like a ballet at the Alhambra,
isn't it? At least, they tell me they're
something like that."

No one was kind enough to gratify his
lordship by the suggestion that the ballet
of the Alhambra was as familiar to him as
—say, the House of Lords.

" We are going to shoot a bit of covert round Barker's cottage for your edification now," Lord Morningham said to Mrs. Welbeck. " This is the covert."

He set the guns in their places, saying that he would find a stand for himself in the covert, and asking Mrs. Welbeck to accompany him.

" But whom will you go with, dear ? " Mrs. Welbeck asked affectionately of Sybil.

" Oh, I—I'll watch Lord Masterton, if he will let me," she said.

His lordship expressed himself honoured, and Morningham led Mrs. Welbeck through a little wicket-gate opening into the wood.

It was a picturesque covert. Far back, where the beat was to commence, the trees were lofty, oaks and firs intermingling. But further on the oaks thinned out, and the firs were less tall, until at the end, whither Lord Morning-ham led his companion, they were for the most part but some three or four times a man's height. All the "guns," except the one in the corner, stood in the open field two gunshots or more from the trees, so as to give the pheasants making for another covert behind the sportsmen a chance of rising before coming to the " guns."

The day had now grown bright and clear, and the pheasants were likely to fly high and fast. As Lord Morningham and Mrs. Welbeck threaded their way through the hazel undergrowth, they came upon a man gently tapping with his stick upon a tree-stem. This was one of the "stops' stationed to prevent the pheasants from running across to the other covert before the "guns" should have taken their places. Upon their approach this man, acting upon previous instructions, went away.

About twenty yards from the edge of the wood the trees grew thinner, with none too wide intervals in which a quick gun might get a shot.

"This will be about the best place, I think," Lord Morningham said.

Behind them, at a discreet distance—at a distance, that is to say, at which he could hear what they were saying, while they should imagine him to be out of earshot—stood Morningham's loader, with two guns and a cartridge bag slung upon his back.

"You will want a seat, Mrs. Welbeck, I

am sure you must be tired," Lord Morningham suggested.

"Oh no, indeed I'm not," she answered.
" I'd much sooner stand."

"Oh no; but I must insist upon it," he
urged. "Just go down to Lord Masterton,"
he said to his loader, "in the far right of
the line, he is; and give him my compli-
ments, and ask him if he would have the
goodness to lend Mrs. Welbeck his shooting stick seat for this drive."

"Oh, that's the idea, is it?" said the
golden lady. "I did not quite understand."

"It's rather a good idea, isn't it?"
Morningham asked, with a smile, as he
watched the loader wearily climbing, under
his weight of guns and cartridges, over
the fence, and on to the plough.

" Yes, it is," she assented, with a laugh. " You are growing quite clever. It is a pity though, that Lady Morningham is with Lord Masterton. You know she probably wants to sit down a great deal more than I do really."

" Oh, she's all right," Lord Morningham said carelessly.

" You don't treat your wives with any great *politesse,* you English husbands ; the French are much more polite, even if less devoted."

" Do you think I don't treat my wife well ? " he asked.

" Oh ! " said Mrs. Welbeck, with a lift of the eyebrows and the shoulders, " *Cela dépends.* I think you are somewhat distant in your manner with her, my dear. It would not quite do for me—with a devoted husband."

"She is a good wife to me," he said coldly, as if rather resenting the comparison, and his companion's tone. "But how about Mr. Welbeck?" he went on. "Are you so truly and faithfully and eternally attached to him?"

"Oh, our's was only a *mariage de convenance* from the very first," she said. "It has so been understood on both sides. And I must say," she added, with a merry laugh, "we have both been very true to that clause of the contract at all events. But oblige me, my dear, will you," she went on more seriously, "by being a little less cold and distant in manner to your wife. Do this, please—in public, I mean —I do not request that you are to fall in love with her. But in public—if you treat her so—it might, you know—it might almost make some people disposed to blame me!—and to say that—people are so absurd—you cared for me—cared for me more than you do for her, you know! What? isn't it absurd?"

"Folly!" he said; "as if you didn't know that everyone says so already!"

Then his tone changed. "You are a witch!" he exclaimed passionately. "I believe you are—to make me love you so. A witch or an angel—I am not sure which."

"Oh, say the latter, please, my dear; it sounds so much nicer," she answered, laughing merrily. "Lord Morningham in love with an angel! How sweetly ethereal. But remember what I have asked you, and hush! your loader in coming back."

The shooter chose a spot where a tree on his left eclipsed the dazzle of the sun.

The servant loaded the guns, handed one
to his master, and held the other in readi-
ness ; and the pleasure of the sport began
—in its expectation.   The tapping of the
distant beaters' sticks could be faintly
heard.   Occasionally a jay scolded with
harsh profanity.   The pheasants running
in the covert began to patter audibly
with their feet on the dry leaves.   One
came skimming over, low-flying—too low
to shoot—rising suddenly upward as he
caught a glimpse of the waiting trio.   A
blackbird scudded towards them among
the trees, quickly diving out of sight to
the left, with a chuckle of terror.   The
running pheasants began to appear—
stopping short at view of their enemies,
and standing for a minute as still as if
they were stuffed, with black, beady eye

all agaze ; then, lowering their heads, ran
back again. A hare came cantering con-
tentedly, thinking he had left his troubles
behind him. The sportsman fired, the
hare rolled over, gave a kick or two,
splashing up the leaves, and died. There
was a great noise of the pheasants, terrified
by the shot, scuttling back. Then came
another hare at full headlong gallop, close
past them. The shooter turned, fired
through the underwood, at the galloping
creature, and he too rolled over and lay
still. A jay appeared over the fir trees ;
the sportsman half raised his gun, but,
before he could fire, the jay dropped back,
with a scold, below the horizon. Then,
between the tree tops came a quick,
scudding pheasant—too quick for the
shooter.

"Missed him clean!" he exclaimed;
"it's sharp work."

Another pheasant followed with almost
identical flight.   At the shot his head
seemed to stop moving, and be overtaken
by his body.   Then he fell with slanting
crash through the trees.

"Got him that time," said Lord Morningham grimly.

A jay appeared like his predecessor, but
attempted the same tactics of retreat a
moment late, for, turning with the gun he
was just handing to his loader, the shooter
killed him with his second barrel.

The sportsmen in the field began to be
busy.   With a great whirring of wings, a
big rise of pheasants rocketed into the air.
"Bang! Bang!" and then again, "Bang!
Bang!" with his second gun, went the

shooter in the covert, and three pheasants were falling dead at the same moment.

" Missed that last," he said.

And " Bang! Bang!" often reiterated, went the party in the field; and where Mrs. Welbeck stood she could see now one and now another high rocketer cease its flight, and come whirling, windmill-wise, or falling stone dead, downwards.

Hares kept galloping past, one affording a shot, another eluding it—only visible in glimpses through the undergrowth. Pheasants kept streaming over—a select few crashing downwards to the shot—the majority escaping, not fired at. A few dodging rabbits met their doom—more broke back between the beater's legs, a few were killed by their sticks as they tried to break the cordon.

At length the beaters came up close. The shooting was confined to an occasional shot at a pheasant rising and going back. It was all over. Now for the gathering and the numbering of the slain.

" How many was it, I wonder ? " Lord Morningham said. " I counted thirty-two. There were one or two I couldn't be sure of. It's a good stand, but very quick shooting."

The beaters and keepers and an eager retriever or two went in to hunt among the covert, and Mrs. Welbeck and Lord Morningham joined the party in the field, where the pheasants were being gathered and laid out in a long row About a hundred pheasants, two partridges, a few hares and rabbits, a woodcock, a wood-pigeon, and three jays, was the satisfactory total of the beat.

The game was hung up it the game-cart, which now bore somewhat the appearance of a travelling larder. The ladies got into the omnibus and started homewards, while the gentlemen trudged away over the plough to take their places for a partridge drive.

CHAPTER VI.

THE HOUSE PARTY.

THE everlasting pursuit of social pleasure, the sleeplessness, the chloral, above all, the strain of her self repression, were wearing down Sybil's splendid health. No one but herself knew it, but she lived in perpetual fear of a nervous crisis. Sometimes she would be lying in the depths of a great arm-chair in her little room, gazing into the fire and weaving wonders in the embers, when an influence not born of any vision she saw there would seize her. Every nerve would be tingling. She

(86)

would raise herself from the chair and, trembling in all her limbs, would gaze around the room with relief, in which disappointment mingled, to find no visible justification of her emotion. She began to find herself inadequate company. She felt even her husband's presence a support in her nameless fears, though she never spoke of them to him. Those hours between the time at which she sent her maid to bed and that at which Lord Morningham came up from the smoking-room, if they were in the country, or from a club or elsewhere in London, were a torture to her. She passed them in cowering fits of nervous tremor. At times she would get out of bed and light all the candles. Then, she would fancy that they threw uncanny shadows, and would put them all out, keeping only her night lamp burning. But the darkness, and above all, her dreams, would be peopled with shapes infinitely worse than the suggestions of the flickering candles, and again she would get up and rekindle the illumination. But she did so reluctantly, and in fear of her husband's coming, for Lord Morningham, like many men of his temperament whose expenditure is large and income yet larger, was the slave of small economies, and in his measured, deadly manner found fault with the waste and folly. To others she could return sarcasm for sarcasm, and defeat them with their own weapons, but the only weapon that she now had against her husband was his favourite and least aggressive one of icy silence.

On the evening of the day of the shooting lunch at Barker's cottage, the drawing of the lots again gave Lord Morningham his golden lady to take to dinner.

"I have been obedient to your behest," he whispered to her. "I have telegraphed to Garraud's for a necklace of pearls I lately saw there, for her ladyship. Will that have a good effect, do you think? I will request her to wear them at dinner to-morrow, and will draw attention to them."

"What a devoted spouse," said the golden lady archly.

It had been Robert's fortune to draw Lady Morningham. He talked fitfully, but for the most part was silent and thoughtful. He was distrustful of himself. He asked himself if he had done wisely in coming here and putting himself under the same roof with one who had been,

who still was, though she was now another's
wife, so very much to him.   For he found
that his heart was not dead, as he had
believed it to be, to this great life passion ;
and he had divined too, that which Sybil
thought to be her own secret, the unhappiness and the starved emptiness of her lot.
The knowledge made him wonderfully
gentle and tender in his manner to her,
and by his very reserve drew her closer
to him.   But he knew the peril, and resolved that on the morrow he would plead
pressure of business and expose himself to
it no longer.

With this determination, his mind became
more at ease, and he talked in his natural
manner.   His talk was very good, for it
had a range of many subjects which he
knew intimately and had thought out

originally—that is, with an originality
quickened by Mr. Fleg. Mr. Fleg had
taken nearly all intellectual knowledge as
his province, and with the Flegian encyclo-
pedia as his companion, Robert had spent
two years of travel in the country best
adapted to make thought active. And
this thought Mr. Fleg had trained to work
on logical methods. The side of humanity
with which Mr. Fleg was least akin, was
the side with which Robert had most
natural sympathy—the artistic side. So
that, by sheer force of circumstances, Robert
found himself wonderfully well equipped
with the elements that go to form the
complete conception of the man *teres atque
rotundus*. He could scarcely have been
otherwise, nor thus equipped could his
talk fail to interest.

After dinner, the gentlemen paid a brief visit to the drawing-room. Then the ladies said good night, and the men were soon gathered in the billiard-room in the glorious unrestraint of smoking suits and slippers.

Lord Morningham presently left them. " I'm off early to-night," he said. " Will the last man please ring the bell, and tell them to put out the lights."

Some said good night, others contented themselves with a nod. Two of the party were playing billiards, and the rest were chatting round to the accompaniment of the click of the balls and exclamations of " Fluke !" " Hard lines !" " Good stroke !" evoked by incidents of the game. On a side table were some corpulent stone bottles, holding spirits, and various kinds of effervescent waters, also cigars and cigarettes. Presently Robert Burscough strolled up to another side table on which were bedroom candles and matches, and, lighting one of the candles, went towards the door.

" Hullo, Burscough ! you off too ? " asked one of them.

" No ; I'm only going to the drawing-room to look for a book," he said.

The gas in the drawing-room had been turned off, but Robert was surprised to find, as he opened the door, that the room was not altogether without light. There was a slight murmur of voices and a sound of movement as he came in, and he saw Mrs. Welbeck and Lord Morningham engaged in a zealous search for some volume in the revolving bookcase.

"It must be here somewhere," said Mrs. Welbeck, rather too loudly.

"Yes, it certainly must be here somewhere," echoed Lord Morningham, in much the same tone.

"What is it that you are looking for?" Robert asked.

"Oh, it's—it's 'Pécheurs d'Ilande.' I know I had it here before dinner," Mrs. Welbeck said.

"Yes, I happened to notice it in your hand when I wished you good night; you carried it upstairs," Robert said in his even voice. "What a charming book it is, is it not? Such a touching picture of how faithfully devoted a wife can be—to even the memory of a husband."

"Did I really take it upstairs? I dare say I did, after all. How stupid of me!

Well, I ought not to grumble since it has given me the pleasure of saying good night to you again, Mr. Burscough. Good night, Lord Morningham."

"Do you believe in woman suffrage, Morningham?" Robert asked, as soon as Mrs. Welbeck was gone.

"Well, from what I can gather from the feeling of the house of Peers," Lord Morningham began; but he stopped abruptly. "Why do you ask?" he said.

"If women were to go into Diplomacy, there very soon would not be a man in the Diplomatic Service," Robert said.

Lord Morningham smiled coldly appreciative. "Have you got your book? Come down to the smoking-room and have a cigar," he suggested. "I meant to go to bed, but I think I shall first smoke a cigarette."

They passed the billiard-room, with its click of balls and hum of voices, and went down to the quiet little smoking-room, where they were soon settled before a good fire, each in an easy chair. For some while they sat in silence, pursuing their separate trains of thought, forgetful of the other's presence. Then Robert, as if the thread of his reflections led him to his companion, slowly turned his head and pursued his reverie, with his eyes bent in reflective study upon Lord Morning-ham's pale, worn face. Morningham, self-absorbed, did not notice his scrutiny, but continued to gaze into the fire, whose restless flame played strange games of light and shadow with his features.

He started when Robert at length spoke.

"Morningham, what's your view about the relation of the sexes?"

"View! It's rather a large question," he said.

"Perhaps I'd better put it in a concrete form. I'll put it to you as an imaginary case. I, we'll say, am in love with a woman—or imagine I am, at least—I make love to her at all events, and the trouble is, you see, that she is another man's wife."

"And the other man has discovered it, do you mean?"

"No," said Robert; "I'm supposing that he hasn't found it out."

"Well, what's the trouble, then? He suspects it, do you mean?"

"No, I'm supposing that he does not

suspect it the least in the world, that he
is perfectly unaware of it, and trusts me
and his wife perfectly. Don't you think
a fellow would feel rather a cur about it
then ? "

Lord Morningham smiled in his own
manner—his habitual smile suggestive of
malevolence. " In these days," he said,
" every one makes love to his neighbour's
wife ; it is well understood. It is the
thing to do."

" Is that your view of it, really ? "

" Well, yes, if you ask me, I suppose it
practically is. Of course, it is distinctly
immoral, and so forth ; but one must be
guided by the rules of the society one
lives in, and it is certain that this is not
a very grievous sin in the eyes of that
society. It's not nearly so bad, for

instance, as wearing a wrong-shaped hat or not knowing the right sort of people."

"Yes, I know. Of course that's the way it is looked at. But it's all very wrong, don't you think so?" Robert asked, with curious naïvete, as the other thought.

"Well, it is and it isn't," said Morningham, in the satisfactory way of one who conveys a final truth. "I mean that by the rules of abstract morality it is wrong, of course, but judged by the code of the society in which one moves, it is not at all wrong, provided the discovery be not too flagrant, and as a member of that society one must be guided by its code. If not, where is one? One is either without a code at all, or one must go away and live in another society."

"Yes, I know all that, of course. But supposing that the man was a friend of your own, that you accepted his hospitality. Should you not deem that that would make a difference?"

"Well, I really don't see that it would. What I think is this: when a man makes love to another man's wife, he does it at his own risk—that is all. If he is caught, he must expect to have his brains blown out I take it, or if it does not quite come to that, to be severely castigated, physically or financially. A man knows that, and, as I say, he does it at his risk."

Robert turned in his arm-chair with a movement of intense repulsion. "But, look here, Morningham," he said. "Just consider it seriously. Put yourself for a moment in the other man's place. Suppose a man whom you fully believed to be your friend—suppose *I*, for instance, were to make love to *your* wife (forgive me, but it seems the only way of bringing it home to you), would you not think me a mean, despicable scoundrel if you were to find me out ?"

"Well, no, Burscough, I don't think I should think that exactly, but I think I should be disposed to try to make it uncomfortable for you ; that is all."

"And these are your real honest opinions in these matters ?"

"Yes, they are, indeed ; and what's more, you'll find them very serviceable opinions to get along with. I do," he concluded, with a very evil laugh. "And now, if you will excuse me, I'm going to see what they are doing in the billiard-room."

The many-sided product of the Flegian system seldom swore, but now, while he stood with his back to the fire and his hands in his pockets, watching the slowly retreating figure of his host as though it were some natural curiosity, he said with a slow solemnity which carried weight, " Well, I'm d——d !"

CHAPTER VII.

WHEN Lord Morningham at length went upstairs, he found Sybil's room in one of those phases of illumination which always irritated him. It was not only the wasteful expenditure to which he objected, but the bright light gave him a momentary sense of physical discomfort.

"What nonsense this is," he said in a rough manner, which discredited his intellectual training, going to one light after the other and extinguishing it.

Sybil came towards him in a dressing-

(103)

robe. "Stay a moment," she said, as he stretched up his hand to one of the candles. "Thank you—yes—I see," she added in a colourless tone, a moment later.

"What do you see?" he asked, as he went on with his work of putting out the candles.

She did not answer. She had crept into bed; and her husband did not trouble himself to question her farther.

Neither did she respond when he spoke to her in the morning; but he took little notice of it. In this respect he often had to accommodate himself to her manner.

When he went downstairs he found his letters in the breakfast-room, and with them was the necklace for which he had telegraphed to Garraud's. After breakfast he took up the jewels to his wife's room. She was in a loose wrapper, seated before the glass, with the maid brushing her beautiful dark hair. Her face was very pale.

" Here is the necklace," he said, " which I told you I had seen at Garraud's. I telegrahed for it yesterday."

" You may go, Palmer," she said to the maid. " I want to talk to his lordship."

She watched the door close behind the maid, whose manner of going was full of protest. Then she turned slowly round. She took the beautiful string of heavy, even pearls from the jewel-case, which her husband had laid open on the toilet table, and without a word flung them full in his face. Then she threw herself upon the bed, and lay there, face down, making the whole bed shake with convulsive sobs. The long pent-up fever of her agony had broken forth tempestuously.

Lord Morningham stood a moment in speechless amazement. The actual blow of the heavy jewels, which he had received full in the face, was no light one, but was as nothing compared to his astonishment at his wife's action.

"Will you kindly explain to me the meaning of this insanity?" he asked with deadly composure.

Sybil did not answer. The sobs still shook her frame.

"What does it mean, I ask again. I command you to tell me," he said, holding her quivering shoulder in his grasp.

The touch of his hand gave her strength. She turned on her elbow, choking down her sobs. At sight of his face, her tears dried into a hard glitter.

"Yes, I will tell you," she answered, with a fierce fighting look that was not so very far from suggesting the insanity he had attributed to her. "It means that I am tired of this pretence—this cold and thin pretence game we play. I hate you. You do not hate me, but you find me your useful chattel. Otherwise I am only indifferent to you. It was but last night when you came up that the shoulder of your smoking jacket had face-powder upon it. Really," she said, with a scornful laugh, "your practice should have made you more perfect. I should have thought there was little you have left unlearnt. But I do not mind that—no. I am well broken by this time to that sort of thing; but that you should come to me with a smiling face, with a string of bright stones, and give them to me like a toy to a child, as if you pretended to care anything for my happiness—that you should insult me so—that is what I cannot bear. Go now ; take your pearls, give them to Mrs. Welbeck, and tell her to be a little less generous with her face-powder." She turned upon the bed again and buried her face.

It was a conclusion of ridiculous feminine bathos. Lord Morningham smiled his malevolent, cold sneer at it. Could this really be his wife whom he had known so long of statuesque beauty, and brilliant, keen intellect ? The spectacle of her broken misery was not altogether displeasing to him. He stood silent, appreciating it.

"Oh, for heaven's sake, leave me!" she exclaimed, without raising her head. "If you knew how you were torturing me by your presence, I think even you would go."

He still stood irresolute.

"Oh, do go," she said, raising her head again. "If you knew how I loathed you, you would go."

And he went. He left the pearls lying on the floor, and going to his dressing-room, looked in the glass to see if his face were disfigured by the blow. The mark was scarcely noticeable, and he went down to breakfast with perfect composure.

Presently Robert came in. His dress was a contrast to the shooting clothes of the rest of the party.

"Hullo, Burscough," one of them remarked, "you look painfully respectable."

"I am afraid I do," he assented. "I am very sorry, Morningham, but I have to be off to-day.   It's about that report I told you of.   I find they want it sooner than I had expected.   The 3.15 train will do, if you can send me in."

"Certainly," Lord Morningham said; "but must you really go?   Can you not let the affairs of the nation slide for once?"

But Robert was stedfast.

"I'll come out to luncheon though, if I may; you are shooting near the house, are you not?"

The shooters strolled out to take their first stand for the home coverts, which were mainly the ornamental shrubberies of the house and garden.   Robert went to his room, and successfully defying the inroads of aggrieved housemaids, wrote hard at his report. A little before one, he started in the direction of the sounds of a well-sustained fusillade. As he passed along the terrace in front of the house he was suddenly aware of Sybil standing in the quaint window place of her favourite room. She was leaning, in a reverie, against the closed lattice, with her forehead pressed upon the pane. He stopped, and made a half movement of retreat, but at the same instant she caught sight of him. He came to the window to wish her good morning, but she could not hear him through the glass, and drew back the window. It opened nearly to the ground, and he stepped in. He was shocked by her paleness, but thought it kinder to forbear comment. They sat, each on a side of the window in the square backed seats.

Now this had been Sybil's dream of days, of weeks, of months, that they should be sitting thus—he there, she here. And it had come to pass. And now that it had come to pass, of what profit was it ? What did he say—what could he have said, without wrong—that could feed her starved heart ? They returned inevitably to the old days, and again in fancy went, hand in hand, over the remembered places, and recalled the bygone meetings and conversations. But there was one meeting and conversation to which, by tacit consent, neither referred—their walk to the mound, which they called the Viking's tomb, in the wonderful pine wood. And all the while Sybil was marvelling at the man—how he could sit before her and talk to her so, as if she had never done him a great wrong.

She marvelled that if he spoke to her at all it was not to rail on her for her falseness. She longed to tell him all, and she argued to herself that it could be no wrong thing for him to know ; but at the point her courage failed her, and he opened the window again, and went out to join the shooting party at their luncheon.

He met them as they were finishing off the last beat of the morning. Then a spring-cart, which had been in waiting, was summoned, the provisions lifted out, along with a folding table and two folding benches. The loaders wrapped their respective masters in ulsters, and the party were soon seated under the covert's shelter at a meal which it did not need a sportsman's appetite to enjoy.

" You might have shot this morning,

Burscough," Morningham said.   " Why
didn't you do that ? "

"Well, I don't know ; I'm going to
give it up, I think."

"Give up shooting ?   Altogether, do
you mean ?   What in the world are you
going to do that for ? "

Robert laughed, slightly nervously.
" It's just that I don't altogether care
about it, if you want to know.   I enjoy it
well enough while I am at it.   I have
enough of the savage left it me for that,
or enough vanity to be pleased by my skill
when I make a good shot—put it which
way you like.   But then, you know, when
one comes in and is just sitting down to a
good dinner, and feeling happy and comfortable then one is apt to have a vision
of a poor wounded beast or bird cowering

under some ditch or another in the cold, with a dozen little lead pellets somewhere in its works. That is what takes away all the pleasure of it to me. I feel that I am a cruel, selfish brute. I have shot with that feeling often, but I am sure, having that feeling that it is wrong for me to shoot. I am not preaching, mind you (please do not think that), but for me personally, having that feeling, I am sure it is wrong."

"That's true enough, as you put it," Morningham said. "It doesn't do to think too much about this sort of thing certainly."

"Doesn't it?" Robert answered drily. "That seems to be your way of getting over most of the problems of life."

"It is the way I have adopted, since I have come to years of discretion. There was a time when I did otherwise. It is far the best way to enjoy life. That is what is mainly the matter with the world now—that it takes things too seriously."

"I shall be late for my train if I don't take that a little more seriously," said Robert, laughing; and after a hurried hand-shaking all round, he started off at a trot towards the house.

"That young man's chock full of the most extraordinary uncomfortable Utopian ideas," said Lord Masterton, as he smacked his lips over the orange brandy. "Some of you young fellows should just take him in hand, and laugh him out of them."

When Robert reached the house, he found a dog-cart waiting at the front door. His luggage was already in, and his

servant was standing expecting him with
his ulster and stick.

"In a minute," he said as he hurried in.

The ladies were still in the dining-room
lingering over luncheon. He shook hands
with each, coming last to his hostess.

"And you will come and see us in
London, will you not?" Sybil said, as
she expressed conventional regrets at his
going.

"Certainly I will, if I may," he answered;
and, with that, he was off.

After dinner, when the ladies had gone
upstairs and Lord Morningham was in his
dressing-room changing his evening clothes
for a smoking suit, Sybil knocked at the
door.

"If you have no objection," she said,
as she entered, "I shall write to the people

we were going to next week and say that I do not feel well enough, and that you will go alone."

"Are you really unwell?" he asked, without looking at her.

"May I write as I have said?" she asked again, ignoring his question.

"Certainly, if you wish it."

"Thank you; and may I ask Helen Athelstane to come and stay with me?"

"What is the meaning, may I ask, of this new *rôle* of humility? It is unlike you."

"I am unlike myself," she said, with a bitter little laugh. "May I ask Helen Athelstane?"

"You may ask the devil, if you like." Her calmness had exasperated him beyond even his control.

"Thank you!" she said again.

After breakfast the next morning, however, he came into her room, where she was writing, and said abruptly—

"I wish you to accompany me in these visits. It is all nonsense about your being ill, is it not? Have you written to Mrs. Athelstane yet?"

"Yes; there is the letter," she replied; and as she spoke, she took up a closed envelope directed to Mrs. Athelstane, and threw in on the fire.

"Very well," said Lord Morningham, watching her action; "it is understood then that you accompany me?"

"Yes, perfectly," she answered; and turned to her other correspondence.

The following morning the party broke up. The guests departed in the omnibus and broughams, followed by several flies piled with their luggage and packed with their men-servants and maid-servants. Lord Morningham also went up to London, saying he would be back on the Monday ; and Sybil, to her unspeakable relief, was left alone, save for the child and the servants.

When the last of the carriages had gone, she went to the nursery. The baby was asleep. She told the nurse she might go away, and sat down beside the child's cot. She looked at the tiny edition of her own flesh and blood in a coldly contemplative way. She did not bend over it with softly caressant murmurs, touching its forehead with a kiss so gentle that her lips could scarcely feel the contact, as a few days back she would have done. After she had sat there a little while, the baby awoke and began a low fretful cry. She called to the nurse and left the room.

She went about the house, and for a walk in the afternoon, utterly without object. The illustrated weekly papers came and she looked at the pictures, but, when she tried to read the letterpress it did not seem to have any meaning. She comprehended the sentences as she read, but a moment after her memory had lost them.

The nurse asked if she should bring the child to the drawing-room before dinner; but Sybil said no—that she would come and wish her good night in the nursery. She looked in at the nursery for a minute only, said a few words in a baby language to the child, and wished her "tata" without kissing her.

On Sunday she did not go to church ; neither for the last day or two had she said her morning and evening prayers—a habit which she had preserved long after it had ceased to be anything more, and which she had never neglected. She did not seek to occupy herself, and read nothing but her letters all day, nevertheless the hours did not seem long, and she was surprised by the quick succession of meals and the arrival of bedtime.

The next day Lord Morningham came back, and on the following Tuesday they started on a round of visits. For nearly a week Sybil had hardly seen her child. She waved it a cold "tata" shortly before the carriage started. She had not kissed it for several days. But at the last moment, as the carriage was already driving round, and she and Morningham were in the hall with their travelling things on, she suddenly rushed upstairs, bent, with heaving bosom, over the baby's cot, kissed the astonished little creature once, with a kind of wild fervour, and was out of the nursery and down again beside her husband in the hall almost before he had missed her.

They visited three country houses in succession. A large shooting party was collected at each. At each Lord Morningham was bothered by the same often repeated remark, " How ill Lady Morningham is looking."

" Oh no," he always said, in answer ; " she is quite well really. She often looks so. It is nothing."

At the end of a fortnight they went home. In a day or two they were to start again for another round of visits. But even her husband could no longer affect to ignore the change in Sybil's appearance. She ate scarcely anything, and was so pale and thin that her face seemed to have shrunk away to half its size and to have left just two great star-like eyes. Besides, it bothered him to have people continually remarking on her appearance. He used to say to himself, in the tone of an injured person, that it seemed like a personal reproach to himself.

So, when Sybil said, " I am afraid you will have to go on these visits alone; I fear I am really not well enough," he agreed without demur.

The day before he went, she said, " I

have asked Helen to come and stay with me while you are away."

" Indeed," he answered ; " you were not good enough to tell me of your intention. I think that I might have expected that much consideration in my own house."

" The last time," said she in a perfectly indifferent way, as if she were mentioning a fact of no personal interest—" the last time when I asked you if I might ask her, you sneered at what you called my humility."

Lord Morningham for once was at fault for an answer, and went out with something very like an oath on his lips.

CHAPTER VIII.

FILIAL INGRATITUDE.

"THE Braes o' Mar" were going merrily. The Fish Company still had a nominal existence, but as a source of profit to its estimable directors it was no more. Young Cheadle's petition had been granted. The Company was in liquidation. Under the order of Court, a general meeting had been held to discover the true wishes of the shareholders, which the Board in certain affidavits had greatly misrepresented. Further, the judge had granted an order for the cross-examination of the Board on their affidavits.

(126)

The directors had not anticipated the cross-examination order. Hitherto both Mr. Cheadle and the Semitic gentlemen on the Board had enjoyed excellent health. They had not even had the influenza. But, immediately upon this order, a sudden and severe epidemic attacked them. They were compelled to go to the seaside in search of natural tonics, to see what ozone would do for them, and wrote enclosing a doctor's certificate and expressing their extreme regret that their state of ill health was such that a journey to the metropolis would be attended with great risk.

The date of the meeting ordered by the Court arrived, and no cross-examination had been made. The room was densely packed, and there appeared to be a good deal of feeling.

The temper of the meeting exhibited itself as soon as the chairman appointed by the Court referred, in his opening remarks, to Mr. Cheadle and others of the board. Their names were greeted with howls. The meeting was like lions in a Roman amphitheatre, expecting Christians.

The Secretary of the board was on the Chairman's right, recording minutes.

A prominent shareholder obtained leave to put to the Secretary some questions germane to the business on hand. He wished for information relative to the investment of the Association's capital.

"Was it true," he asked, referring to a paper he took from his pocket, "that the Board had invested five thousand pounds in 'The Central Africa and Great Desert of Sahara Railway Company'?"

" Yes."

" Four thousand pounds in ' The Dutch Irrigation Company, Limited ' ? "

" No."

" No," said he, surprised. " Ah yes, I see, I had the title a little wrong. In ' The Dutch and Low Countries' Irrigation Company, Limited ' ? "

" Yes," said the Secretary. " That is correct."

An unusually hungry howl greeted the subterfuge of the Secretary.

" Two thousand five hundred pounds in ' The Dead Sea Fisheries Company, Limited ' ? " the shareholder continued.

" Yes," said the Secretary.

" Four thousand pounds in ' The Icelandic and Faroe Islands Submarine Telegraphic Company, Limited ' ? "

" Yes," said the Secretary.

" Well, gentlemen," the prominent shareholder said, holding up his paper and
addressing the meeting; "we may all be
very proud, I am sure, of the undeniable
securities in which the Board, our trustees,
have invested our capital.   One and all of
these Companies, I may inform you, are
the children of that beneficent mother,
the International Investment Company,
Limited, which is also the parent of our
Metropolitan Fish Consumers' Association,
and which is so largely represented on our
board that it and the parent board are
almost identical."

And the speaker, having made his point
with the meeting, wisely sat down without
blunting it by talk.

Then the votes were taken, and the

voice of the meeting was as of one man demanding that the Fish Company should be wound up by the Court.

So young Cheadle had practically gained his case, but he seemed in no immediate hurry to return to the land of his adoption. His lodgings at Pebblecombe were not luxurious, as most know luxury, but they fulfilled his conception of it. Pipes and tobacco were within reach on the mantelpiece, on which also generally were young Cheadle's feet. At another point his person was supported by a leather-covered arm-chair. The materials for several Transatlantic drinks, with metaphorical names that suggested their attributes, were close at hand. And the furniture of the room was completed, one might say crowned, so important was it in young Cheadle's domestic economy, by a spittoon.

On this scene Mr. Cheadle, senior, entered one fine evening in spring.

"Ah, come in, old man. Is that you?" said the son. "Have a liquor?"

Mr. Cheadle declined, with the air of implying that the passion of thirst was unknown to him.

"My boy," he said affectionately, as he took a seat, "your conduct is grieving me very much."

Young Cheadle chuckled like an old grouse. "Hum!" he said; "yes; I guessed it would."

"I will not discuss with you your view, which I believe to be sadly distorted, of my own action in connection with this Metropolitan Fish Consumers' Association," said Mr. Cheadle, loftily waving aside, with the air of a prime minister, inconvenient personal criticism; "but I will ask you to take a glance at your own action. You are forcing on this cross-examination of members of the board, and I am greatly in hopes that you do not realize the uncomfortable position in which I may be placed by it."

"Oh yes!" said young Cheadle indifferently; "I quite understand it—a month or two's hard labour. Yes, it's uncomfortable I guess, but it's fine exercise. It would do your health a pile of good. That's my first consideration, of course, you know."

" You're a devil!" said Mr. Cheadle.

" Think so?" said his son. "Look at my parentage."

"No, no, no; I beg your pardon," the parent hastened to say. He had not come to wrangle, but to beg. He returned to his *rôle* of suppliant *in forma pauperis.* "I do not ask you to consider me," he went on, with a touching self-abasement; "but I would ask you to consider the name you bear, our family, your sainted mother."

Young Cheadle's usual manner was nonchalant and nasal. He seldom changed it. When he did, the alteration was so much the more startling.

"Stop!" he said, springing out of his arm-chair, and glaring at his father so hard that the very force of the glance nearly knocked Mr. Cheadle backwards. "Stop! If you introduce my mother's name into your fictions, I won't leave much of you to do hard labour with, when this fish business is cleared up."

Mr. Cheadle was full of an idea that people who came from America had a nasty way of concealing derringers and bowie knives on their persons. He was a man of peace, and his son's eye betokened war. He hastened to make the soft answer that turns away wrath, and promised that the name of the late Mrs. Cheadle should be sacred. He went back to his old ground, the credit of the family name. Upon which young Cheadle turned the occasion to account, and expounded to his parent his views of social morality. He did this less with the purpose of that parent's regeneration (he was rather inveterate) than of explaining his own position.

"Well, now," he said, "it's this very point of the family credit that has made me take the action I have. You see our views differ. It appears to me that the right thing for the family credit is that the family should act honestly, and do nothing to discredit it. Your idea of what you talk about as the family credit—though you do not care about it two cents—is to do all the dirty, mean tricks you can, and hide them all away. That's where we differ. And it seems to me," said young Cheadle, with an emotion that was rare in him, "that it's my view of the case that that dear woman, my mother, will take, looking down upon us from heaven. Anyway, my intention is this—to proceed with this action, and to go against the directors personally for the funds they have made

away with. But I don't want you to suffer.
After all, you are my father, and my
mother's husband, though every one connected with you has reason to be ashamed
of you. You are our misfortune, and we
have to make the best of you. Now, the
best thing that can happen to you is this
—you shall give me an undertaking,
guaranteeing me, to the full extent of your
property, if necessary, against the money
I shall have to pay to square with your
friend that you have robbed. I mean
Colonel Burscough; the smaller shareholders don't matter. Then you shall
clear out of the country and go to America,
where my agent will take care of you.
And if you don't do that, I'll proceed
against you personally and criminally."

It was a very sad situation for poor Mr.

Cheadle. Was ever filial ingratitude more inhumanly manifested? All this he had brought on himself by his munificently prodigal generosity in planting this awful son in a spot in America where dollars seemed to have grown like daisies from the soil. Mr. Cheadle had every right to deem himself one of the most ill-used of men. He tried once more upon his strong-hearted offspring the appeal *ad misericordiam.*

" Think of all I have done for you," said the parent. " I have fed you, clothed you, schooled you, started you in America on the road to a splendid fortune."

" Stop !" said the son. " We have squared all that; you have my cheque. To America you shall go, or, if you stay at home, you must abide the legal proceedings."

He explained, however, that he was not wedded to the scheme of being at the cost of maintaining his parent in America. He offered him that refuge out of his royal bounty; for there his agent would look after him, house him, board him, etc. If he liked, he might go elsewhere (his son would much prefer that he should); but out of England he must go. It did not occur to Mr. Cheadle to ask the name of his son's agent, neither did his son inform him of it. But young Cheadle grinned appreciatively, as he thought of the meeting.

" But look at my interests in this country, in Pebblecombe itself even," Mr. Cheadle pleaded pathetically.

" I will buy them off you at a valuation," said his son inexorably. " And will set the sum to your credit against the sum I have to pay out to one, at least, of the men you have robbed."

"Robbed!" said Mr. Cheadle, with aversion. "It is a nasty word."

"It is," said young Cheadle emphatically, "derned nasty; unfortunately, it's the derned truth."

It was quite an artistic piece of justice. The superfluous son, who had been planted out in America to be a forgotten failure, had come back with a fortune, and was now planting out his superfluous parent in the self-same spot and manner. It recalled the filial piety of the Phœnix.

"But are you not coming out to America yourself?" Mr. Cheadle asked, with a gleam of hope, as he thought of the frailty of human, and Yankee agents.

"Oh yes!" said young Cheadle, smiling in forecast of his parent's thought; "I shall soon be there. Don't be troubled about that—as soon as I have fixed things up here a bit."

Mr. Cheadle departed with "the Braes o' Mar" ringing cheerily in his ears, a Christian "good night" upon his lips; but, at his heart, black bitterness at the ingratitude of sons.

"There is one trifle I should desire to retain and except from your valuation," Mr. Cheadle had said, with heart-rending pathos, as if his son were a bailiff in possession. "It is of no value; and even so, it is not for myself that I ask it. It is Mr. Slocombe's portrait, pained by young Robert Burscough—one of the young man's earliest efforts."

The thing hung in the smoking-room. Technically, it was a daub of the most unredeemed kind—the colour laid on anyhow, the composition nowhere; but the likeness was emphatic, and it was a daub of genius.

Young Cheadle graciously assented to his parent's humble prayer, with a smile at its strange nature.

In the afternoon Mr. Cheadle took the daub of genius from the wall, wrapped it in brown paper, and walked with it under his arm to Little Pipkin.

Mr. Slocombe was at home, and expressed surprise and gratification when he saw his visitor.

They discoursed on topics of universal interest, such as cricket, funerals, and the growth of turf. Occasionally the parrot threw in a pertinent remark. The cricket inevitably led to Robert Burscough, and to the real object of the visit.

"Mr. Slocombe," Mr. Cheadle said solemnly, "I believe I may say that I have never done you a wrong. Is not that so?"

"Done me a wrong, sir! No, that you never have. Nobody never does me no wrong sir, not since I can remember."

Mr. Cheadle looked at him with an expression of respect that was perfectly genuine. He even forebore to tell him that he was a wonderful man.

"Well, Mr. Slocombe," he said instead, "I want you to do something for me. I want you to accept this picture—I know you will value it, though it is not a thing of value in itself—and to hang it on your wall, and to think of me, when you look at it, as a man who has never done you any wrong; because, although you may not know it, there are very few who will ever think of me like that. Good-bye, Mr. Slocombe. We will not have any thanks, if you please."

So Mr. Slocombe put up the daub of genius facing the "Arethusa," off which his son was drowned, in that bottle-green sea; and whenever he looked at it, would shake his head in profound speculation, and say reflectively, in reference to the donor—

"Funny gentleman he be, faith—main kind gentleman, though."

So Mr. Cheadle had his queer wish, and a good man thought of him as one who had done him no wrong.

CHAPTER IX.

DEEP WATERS.

"Why, Sybil dear," said Mrs. Athelstane, as she got out of the brougham and found Lady Morningham awaiting her at the open hall-door, "how wretchedly ill you are looking."

The candour of the words was more than compensated by the sympathy of manner.

"Oh, Helen," Sybil replied, kissing her, "I'm *so* glad you've come."

She clung to her, half crying and half laughing, and led her across the hall into the morning room where the tea was.

"Oh, I'm so glad you've come," she said again, when they were out of sight of butler and footmen.

The other looked at her scrutinizingly. "And how's Morningham?" Mrs. Athelstane asked at length.

"Oh, he's quite well, I think," she replied, turning away her eyes. "He's at the Bartons, you know."

"My poor Sybil!" said Mrs. Athelstane, laying her hand, with a quick sympathetic movement, on her friend's.

The tears came into Sybil's eyes.

"And how's the baby?" the other asked.

"Oh, she's well, quite well. You shall see her soon. But now you must have some tea."

After a while they went to the nursery.

The nurse was walking about the room with the child in her arms, crooning a little baby ditty. Sybil watched while Mrs. Athelstane coaxed and talked to the baby, but herself hardly spoke to the child.

At dinner and in the evening there was a deal to talk about. Although these two were very regular correspondents, there were innumerable questions to ask and to be answered, and finally Sybil took her friend off to sleep with her. When the elder woman knelt beside the bed to say her prayers, Sybil looked at her for a moment, and then went to a chair by the fire.

"Have you said your prayers, Sybil?" Mrs. Athelstane asked, when she had finished her own.

"I! No, Nelly; no, I haven't," she

answered, in a voice that she tried to make indifferent. "Oh no, Nelly, I can't," she said, suddenly breaking down —"I can't say my prayers now. I feel so wicked ; I feel as if every atom of love and good was frozen up in me. I hardly even seem to feel any natural affection for the child, and I used to love her so. Oh, I am so unhappy!" and she burst out crying as if her heart would break.

It was the first word she had said of confession of her sorrow. Mrs. Athelstane had known it, but with wise patience had foreborne to force her confidence. But now she did her utmost to soothe and comfort her, and Sybil went to sleep that night like a wearied child, happier in her friend's sympathy than she had been for weeks past.

The morning following they went for a ride. Sybil had ridden little lately, not feeling disposed to the trouble of putting on her habit to go out by herself or with a groom. But this morning she made up for the past days. The Sheik was fresh, and she in a mood to indulge him. Coming to an open down, she startled him with a sudden sting of her whip, and away they shot over the grass, leaving Helen Athelstane and her staider quadruped gazing in wonder as they followed. On and on Sybil went, till her friend began to fear that the horse was beyond her control, but at length she stopped and turned and gallopped back.

"Oh, that was glorious!" she said, reining the beautiful Arab short back as she came up. "Glorious! Nothing has taken me out of myself for days like that gallop."

She looked splendid, Mrs. Athelstane thought, with her cheeks all aglow with the excitement and the exercise.

" Isn't he a beauty, Helen—my beautiful Sheik ? " she said, patting the bright arching crest, while the horse snorted and caught at his bit responsive to the touch of her hand.

After that, when they came in again, she played with her baby and kissed her, as she used to do before. And when they went to bed, she said—

"You have done me so much good to-day, darling Helen. I can say my prayers to-night."

The days went on, and for some three weeks they heard nothing of Lord

Morningham. Sybil was stronger and brighter.

One afternoon, as they were seated on the sofa together at five o'clock tea, they heard a carriage drive to the door. They speculated which of their neighbours it could be. Suddenly Mrs. Athelstane saw Sybil's eyes take a fixed, scared look. She shrank back into herself, and seemed in some incomprehensible way to grow smaller. Her face paled, and her lips set.

"Helen, it's Morningham," she said, scarcely above a whisper.

In a minute he was in the room, greeting them in his formal way.

"Why, we never heard you were coming," Mrs. Athelstane said.

"No?" he answered, interrogatively.

"How did you get out from the station?"
Sybil asked.

"I drove in the brougham," he said.

"Oh, they knew you were coming
then?"

"Certainly.   I telegraphed for the
brougham."

"Oh, they never told me."

Mrs. Athelstane's husband, for all ·his
fine sounding, royal old Saxon name, was
a plain man of business, and had been in
London all these weeks going to his daily
work in the City.   For the last fortnight
his letters had dwelt with pathetic humour
on the loneliness and perils of his widowed
life.   But Mrs. Athelstane had stedfastly
answered that she would stay with her
friend until Lord Morningham's return,
and her husband had assented with perfect

confidence in her wise, unselfish kindness.

Two happier, better suited people than
these there could not be, nor two who
understood and trusted each other more
fully. There was but one cross in their
lives—that they had no children. To
make up, as it were, Mrs. Athelstane
seemed to live in the lives of innumerable
friends, understanding with perfect charity
all the trouble and temptation which beset
them while it seemed to pass her by. In
the world, and with a full knowledge of
the world, and yet not *of* the world, happy
was the man or woman who could reckon
Mrs. Athelstane as a friend.

Among this fortunate number was Robert
Burscough, of whom she had heard very
much from Sybil before her marriage, but

whose personal acquaintance she had not made until after his return from America. Then they became at once such friends that it seemed to Robert as if he had known her for years, as indeed she had, by Sybil's description, known him.

The day after Lord Morningham's return to White-Cross, Mrs. Athelstane went back to her forlorn spouse in London.

A week later the Morninghams also returned to their town house. Robert came once to call, and twice Sybil saw him at evening parties, but he bowed and seemed rather to avoid than to seek her, as in the crush he could readily do without discourtesy. She was far from well, and her nervous system, under the prolonged strain of her miserable starved life, was continually on the verge of collapse.

But in her thirst for any distraction to take her out of herself, she rushed from one to another of the entertainments of the bye-season.

So a month passed. One night Robert, coming from Westminster, looked in late at a dance in a small private house. He had not expected to meet Sybil, but as he came into the room he saw her waltz past him. It was some weeks since he had seen her so near, and he was shocked by her look—her pallor was so deathly, her eyes so hollow and tired. It was a Monday night. He had spent Saturday and Sunday, as his custom was, with the gallant old Colonel at Little Pipkin, and had seen Slocombe and the parrot, and visited many of the old woodland haunts. His heart felt very tender. When Sybil stopped waltzing, he went to her and asked if he might have a dance. She answered lightly and readily enough that he could have the next. Instead of dancing, however, he said that he had had a tiring day, and asked if she would mind sitting out. They found a comfortable corner, but at first felt a mutual sense of restraint. Robert tried the well worn avenues of the books which had been her companions.

"No," she said, "I have been reading nothing. I have given it all up. It is no use trying, and I have been just giving myself up to distractions, and trying to forget myself if I can."

He looked at her with a most pitiful longing to help her. In truth he had scarcely heard her words, though he had

comprehended their meaning—the same
meaning that he read in the pathetic
weariness of the lines of the eyes and
mouth. Of his own next words he was
equally unconscious.

"My darling, I am so sorry for you!"
He was still gazing at her face. The
rush of hot colour into it startled him into
consciousness. "Oh, what did I say?"
he exclaimed confusedly. "I did not
mean it. Oh yes, I did, though. I did
not mean to say it, but it is true—yes, so
true. What harm to say to you once
what you have known all your life, that
half of my being is given up to you."

"Oh no, don't, don't!" she said faintly.
"Why did you tell me? Oh yes, of
course I do," she said, in answer to a
question he whispered in the midst of her

words. " Yes, I love you. But why did you tell me ? And why have you never come near me all these weeks ? Yes, but you were right though. And now you must never come near me again, now that you have told me—never, never, never !"

Then a couple came into the little side-room in which they were sitting, and ensconced themselves therein, and the atmosphere became oppressive with the mutual wish of each couple that the others were elsewhere.

For a minute neither Sybil nor Robert spoke. Then the latter said, " Come, let us dance," and she rose obediently.

They had danced but one turn, full of mysterious fears and delights, when the music stopped.

" I shall go soon," Robert said, " and I

will call to-morrow. Will you be in about three? Never mind—don't answer," he said, fearing a negative; and after a very few more words, he was gone.

"Oh, I wish he had not told me," Sybil kept repeating to herself many times that night, and yet in her heart she knew that it was not true, but that his telling her had put the whole world in tune for her.

Then a fiend suggested a cruel doubt of his truth. "Did he, in fact, care, as he said? Could he possibly be so generous as to care for her, who must seem to have used him so ill? Was not Mrs. Etheredge's confession, after all, a make-up, and had he not really been faithless? Was he not playing with her heart even now? For how could he love one whom he must deem to have so little faith, such shallowness?"

And Sybil, who was acquiring a genius for self-torture, tossed and rocked over this thought all the night through.

The next day he came. She took him by the shoulders and looked hard into his eyes.

"Tell me," she said, "really, truly, faithfully, do you really love me as you say you do?"

"Do I love you, darling?" he answered steadily. "Have I not loved you, with absolutely unswerving allegiance all my life? And when you married this man, and put yourself out of my reach, I went abroad, and did my utmost to put you out of my heart, and in a measure I succeeded for the time being; but afterwards, when

I came back and stayed at Whitecross, it was all just the very same. Oh, Sybil!" and he turned his head away with a groan, checking his words.

"Oh, but say it, say it!" she cried. "Do not stop. Why have you never said it ages ago?—that I have been false to you, that I preferred a coronet and a man I hated, to the man I had said I loved. Do you remember that evening in the pinewood?"

"Do I remember? But hush, Sybil, hush! You are not to say such things of yourself. I have never upbraided you, have I?"

"No, never; and that's what I hate about it. No; I mean that's what I love you for. Oh, I don't know what I mean, except that you have made me so fearfully happy. Ah, but listen—yes, I have got something to tell you now."

And then she told him the whole history —how she had misinterpreted the words she overheard in Mrs. Etheredge's drawing room ; how she had gone in wilful wickedness to Lord Morningham ; and how Mrs. Etheredge had explained away, on her death-bed, the misconstruction. And when she had done, neither of them were free from tears—happy tears—for though by Sybil's mad act their lives had been severed, it was much happiness to know, after worse than doubt, that they had been true.

For a whole delicious hour he was with her—an hour in which, by mutual, tacit consent, no word was spoken of the sense of the necessity of parting which weighed darkly upon the spirit of each.

And in a day or two he came again, with the resolute air of one who has made up his mind that at any cost the right must be done.

"Dearest," he said very gently, "you know we must not go 'on. Whatever it may cost us, we must part. I believe—I hope—I was not wrong in telling you how I loved you; but it cannot go on. You know it, do you not, that we must part?"

"Yes, yes; I know we must," she said, clinging to him pathetically—"we must part; but, oh, there is so very little in my life, and you have brought so very much into it! You are the whole of it. I do not feel as if I *could* bear to part with you."

Then, with great gentleness, he began to put before her all the arguments showing its necessity; but she interrupted him.

"Yes, yes; I know you are right. We must part; and I will try very hard to be brave about it. But you will bear with me a little when I am weak, will you not? It is so very, very cruel."

So he came to see her again once more —one last time—and then they parted— "for ever," as he said. But she said—

"No, no; don't let us *say* 'for ever,' though we may feel it must be so. It sounds so dreadful to say it."

And he was perforce content to leave it so, and to leave the woman he loved alone in it with no comfort but the knowledge of his love for her.

After the first cruel pain of the parting was over, she was for a few weeks infinitely happier. Her reveries were filled with thoughts of the good, true man she loved, and she found support in the thought of his love for her. But then came back to her the despair of it all— the impossibility that they could be anything to each other. And with the despair arose by degrees the old craving for the drugs of excitement.

One hot, langourous afternoon she put on her things and went out. She took the first hansom she met, and told the man to drive to Westminster Abbey. She entered the cool, great building, and it seemed to soothe her with some of its own peace. She sat behind one of the pillars, and, leaning forward, pressed her burning forehead upon the cold stone.

"Oh, God!" she exclaimed, "if this is

Your house, why will You not come to me and comfort me ?"

But her cry had none of the humility of a petition ; it was of the nature of a reproach, and received no answer. Nevertheless, she went away, after a while, somewhat comforted by the physical relief of the cool and quiet.

She had, moreover, come to a resolution. It was now near two months since she had seen Robert. She would write to him, and ask him to come and see her once again. She was to be but a week more in London, for the doctors had ordered her change of air, and rest and freedom from mental worry—that prescription so easy to make up, so hard to take—and as White-Cross Abbey was undergoing extensive repairs in its drainage and so forth, she had taken a small house at a little place named Tangley, among the Surrey Hills. Helen Athelstane was coming to stay with her, having represented to her good husband that she would be constantly up and down—betweet the country and town.

Lord Morningham preferred to stay in London, for in the House of Peers, as he explained, with a weighty sense of his responsibility as steward of such great gifts, he was occasionally indispensable. Sybil and Mrs. Athelstane and the child would be alone in the little country place.

She hardly knew if she looked forward to the change or no. In some ways the prospect pleased her, but she dreaded the thoughts which she would find no distraction there to banish. Still, come what would, she felt she must see Robert before she went.

She wrote to him, and told him she was leaving London, and that it would be a help and a comfort to her to see him once more.

He came, rather against his better judgment, and she told him all about her plans for the summer and the little house at Tangley.

"And, oh, I should so love for you to come down just once, and see us there!" she said. "It would make us seem so much closer to each other, if I could feel that you were able to think of me in that little house and in that lovely country. It seems as if we were so dreadfully separate when we do not know each other's home surroundings. Do you not think so?"

"Yes, dear; yes, dear," he admitted, with grudging assent. "It would be sweet to be able to think of you, and to picture you in that little country home; but, oh, is it wise, Sybil? Can it do any real good? May it not only make it more difficult? And it is all so wrong and wretched."

"Yes; but just once," she pleaded. "It cannot be any great additional harm—just once more, and I think it will be such a comfort to us in the months to come."

Robert yielded. He was wax in this woman's hands—not only by reason of his love, but also of his deep pity. He seemed so placed that it was impossible to be anything but kind, and yet kindness was cruelty and dishonour.

So Sybil and the child, and a maid and

nurse, went down to Tangley, where they found Mrs. Athelstane and a small household staff, which had preceded them to get the little place in order.

A few days later Robert came to pay his promised visit. It was a lovely day, and the beautiful country in its most gorgeous summer attire. Sybil and Helen were at the little apology for a station to meet him, and they walked up to the Cottage, as they called it, together. Then Sybil took him out, and pointed to him the surroundings of the house. She had roamed through and searched all the haunts, looking forward expressly to her pleasure in showing them to him. She wished that he should see them *all;* that there should be none later discovered after his visit, in which, in his mental picture, he should not be able to share. She felt as if they would be in some subtle way inspired for her by his thought of them. She showed him the secrets of the by-paths between the undergrowth of the hazel copse, taking him to each of her favourite points of view; she led him through the gloomy mystery and stillness of the pine-wood behind the house on to a heather-covered common beyond, which stretched away—variegated with dotted clumps of fir trees, and intersected by glades in which were houses and cultivated lands—to the farthest windmill on the horizon. It was a glorious panorama under the bright summer sky. Here was life and splendour; but there, under the dark pine trees, Sybil found mystery and peace, better suited to her mood.

"It is here you must think of me," she said, "among these dear trees. I shall come here every day."

And when Robert went back in the hot, dusty train to London, it seemed to each of them that this had been a day stolen from some brighter life.

"Oh, Robert," Sybil had said, "I do wish it was not so wrong to see you! I feel a better woman for a while after you have gone; but, then, when I have not seen you for a long time, I get desperate, and strive only to banish all thought. But we must not see each other. I know we must not; but it is very, very hard."

CHAPTER X.

MR. CHEADLE'S EXILE.

YOUNG Cheadle had delivered his ultimatum. But it was not in the nature of things, or of Mr. Cheadle, senior, that it should be accepted as such. He did not so much mind going to America, which suggested a new and unworked field for his energies, but he did not at all like the idea of giving security to his son to cover the loss which he had Quixotically determined to make good to Colonel Burscough.

"Quixotic, by Jove," Mr. Cheadle would

softly observe, when his irritation carried
him a little further than usual. "It is
easy to be Quixotic when he has got
security for it. It is *I* that am Quixotic,
it seems to me—not him, after all."

Mr. Cheadle pointed this out to his son,
and gravely warned him against taking
any credit to himself for generosity on his
part, since he was picking the paternal
pocket for the means. Young Cheadle
whistled "the Braes o' Mar" as a quick
step, and promised to try not to grow self-
righteous.

Mr. Cheadle might quite well have
declined to give his son any security, but
he had visions of a police officer coming
on board the boat, even under the very
shadow of the Statue of Liberty, with a
warrant for his arrest. What with electric

telegraphs and extradition, there is no rest
for the luckless wicked. Mr. Cheadle,
much against his inclination, was obliged
to be good.

He pleaded eloquently, almost pathetically. His son was stony-hearted. He
said he would not give the securities. His
undutiful offspring replied by a threat of
extracting from him security for all possible
legal expenses in addition. He was in an
iron grasp. He consented to go.

He busied himself with realizing, as
quickly as possible, his realizable property.
For the rest, his son undertook to realize
it for him, under a power of attorney.

It was one of Mr. Cheadle's rare gifts
to be able to recognize in others a higher
standard of honour than he was capable of
reaching. He knew he could trust his

son. He deemed it better to conceal from his friends his intention of flitting, and young Cheadle, having possession of the securities, promised not to betray him. Again, he knew he could trust him.

Colonel Burscough was a golfer on a one-eyed and one-armed plan of his own; and as he and his nephew were one day wending their way, golf club in hand, to the links, there was a fly, carrying a hand-bag, at the door of young Cheadle's lodgings. Young Cheadle presently came out and put himself inside the fly. When Robert Burscough questioned him about his destination, young Cheadle, thinking his parent had now a fair start, said—

"Going to Southampton to see my father off—good-bye!"

" Where's he going to ? "

" America. Good-bye."

" America ! What to-day ? "

" Yes ; good-bye."

The fly departed, and Robert Burscough stared. He caught up his uncle.

" I say, uncle, here's a pretty go ; old Cheadle's off to America. I never knew he was going—did you ? "

" To America ! No ; knew he was going to the devil—wish he would make haste about it," the Colonel said.

" Did you say he was going to America ? " the Colonel asked again, when they had gone a few steps.

" Yes," said Robert.

" He's being driven away—that's what it is—he's afraid of this fishy business. Poor Cheadle ! "

They walked on a few steps more. Then the Colonel stopped.

"I tell you what it is. I am sorry for Cheadle. He's the jammedest scamp alive; but jam it all, it's hard to see a man, and an old friend, too, hunted off like this. I parted from him in anger too. I tell you what it is; jammed if I won't go to Southampton after him, and see him off."

"You'll never catch the train, uncle."

"Oh yes, I will," said the Colonel. "Jam it all, boy, what are you talking about? Where's a fly. Hi, here! No, that's a milk cart. Oh, jam it all, never a fly in the world when you want one. What am I to do? Yes, run that way, Robert, and I'll run this, and try to get one."

The Bridgehampton porters were surprised to see a hot, angry man, with one arm, and a golf club, instead of a railway ticket, dashing into the train as it moved off, and when Mr. Cheadle saw the Colonel on board the tender at Southampton, he said, " By Jove !" and tried to go below—too late.

Had his enemy, his one-eyed Cyclopian enemy, come to murder him? His son had evidently betrayed him, Mr. Cheadle thought, for the Colonel still grasped his golf club.

" Cheadle, my old friend," he said ; " I could not let you go like this—leaving us all—until I had shaken you by the hand, and told you that I bear no malice. Why do you go ? Cheadle, we do not bear you malice."

Mr. Cheadle seized the situation in a

moment.   He grasped the Colonel's hand with gratitude that was almost painful.

"My dear old friend!" he exclaimed, in a choked voice. "This is too kind, too generous."

"Oh, jam it all, man, one could not see you go away like this, alone, hounded out, as it were, eh?"

"Ah, they have been hard upon me," said Mr. Cheadle. "I have been wrong. But I have been more sinned against than sinning. They led me further than I knew. But I can tell you this, my old friend," he added, drawing him aside (so that young Cheadle should not overhear) by the hand which he still held—"you will not suffer the loss of one penny, through this unfortunate Association; I have taken measures against that. But," he whispered mysteriously, "do not let him," indicating his son, "know that."

A glance full of emotion and a warmer hand squeeze conveyed Colonel Burscough's meaning that he deemed himself the sharer of the working of Mr. Cheadle's inmost heart.

" He has always been against me," said Mr. Cheadle, again indicating his son; "but," he added, and then stopped as though he restrained himself with difficulty, " he is still my son."

The Colonel's hot and generous heart bled for poor Mr. Cheadle. They talked affectionately, young Cheadle occasionally only interpolating a remark, until the bell rang for the clearing of the steamer. On the tender young Cheadle could see nothing of the Colonel. He looked all

about.   The tender was just moving from
the big, North German Lloyd Liner, when
a frantic, one-armed figure appeared on
the great ship's deck.   The figure swung
a golf club with dangerous energy, and
shouted in a voice of thunder to stop the
tender.   The Colonel was received on
board the tender, hot and hustled, but
bursting with satisfaction and noble senti-
ments.

"I could not let him go like that," he
told young Cheadle.   "From what he
tells me, I fancy your good father, if he
erred, has made a noble recompense.
He has greatly impoverished himself, I
fancy, in doing justice to the sufferers by
this fortunate Fish scheme."

"Think so?" said young Cheadle.
"Well?"

"Well, I am a poor man, my boy, but I could not resist just running to the saloon, and writing your good father a cheque for two hundred pounds. It is little enough, after all the recompense he has paid. But it may help him a bit in his exile."

"Ah, yes," said young Cheadle, slowly and thoughtfully. "Well, Colonel, you're a masterpiece, that's all I've got to say. I wonder are all warm-hearted people fools? You're a masterpiece ; but," he added, a little bitterly, "you're a blamed expensive one to me."

Some months later, when young Cheadle returned to his home beyond the "Rockies," his father received him with benign cordiality. The elder Mr. Cheadle had been living in perfect harmony and mutual satisfaction with his son's agent, the man he had deceived and ruined many years before. Mr. Cheadle was very popular in the neighbouring city. He had already been appointed deacon of an evangelical church. There was no church plate belonging to this establishment, and the accounts were well audited by pious men, who understood their business.

"Every one likes your father," the agent told young Cheadle; "but no one leaves his watch about when he is near."

CHAPTER XI.

DOUBTS AND DIFFICULTIES.

IN the days after Robert's visit, Sybil went many times over the paths by which they had walked together—stopped where they had stopped, and tried to recall, word by word, all their conversation. Not only every day, as she had said she would, but many times a day, spending hours there daily. She tried to take to herself the monotony of the life as an anæsthetic, as before she had excitement. But she was yet to learn that monotony is itself as severe a strain on the nerves as excitement.

(185)

They had been there nearly a fortnight before Morningham found leisure to visit them. He had only run down for the day, he said, and must return to town to dinner. Sybil received him as a hostess might a guest, to whom she is reluctantly obliged to show courtesy, and he accepted the position, as if it were what he wished.

" I suppose you have seen nobody since you have been here, have you ? " he asked, as they went to the drawing-room after luncheon.

"Yes, Robert Burscough has been once," Sybil said coldly, though she felt that her colour was rising.

" Robert Burscough ? For what purpose has he been down here ? "

"To see me, I believe," Sybil replied steadily.

"What do you mean?" Then, as she did not answer, he said, with a certain pomposity of manner, which he often affected with her, "I hope you remember that you made certain vows to me when we were married?"

"You do much to help me to remember it, do you not?" she asked scornfully. "Oh, for heaven's sake," she went on impatiently, "do not let us continue this sickening farce. If you have nothing more to say to me, I am going up to see the—your—child."

Lord Morningham did not answer, and they scarcely addressed each other again during his stay; but this visit of her husband's roused her from the delusion that she was finding peace in the deadness of the monotony. She began again to yearn, with all the old morbid craving, primarily to see Robert ; but if that were not possible without indignity to their mutual resolves, to find distraction in any kind of excitement.   In her wanderings and reveries among the pine-trees she had preferred to be alone, but now she called on her friend, Helen Athelstane, to take long energetic walks, with her, an exercise not greatly to the friend's taste.   Nevertheless, Helen's sympathy was perfect, whether to leave her in solitude or to give her companionship in tearing up and down the Surrey Hills.

But it was all no good.   Though Sybil had at first said to herself that nothing should induce her to write again to Robert, yet after a while she began to confess to herself that it was but a question of days

when she would yield to her ever-growing
need of his presence, and, that once admitted, the day of her yielding of necessity
soon came. The moral weakness was in
part consequence of her physical weakness. In perfect health her will would
have been more resolute. Their isolation
from the world had been very absolute.
Robert and Lord Morningham had been
virtually their only visitors. Some of the
country neighbours had called, and even
had left cards upon them in return ; but
Sybil felt disinclined to make new ac-
quaintances. Thus they had practically
seen no one, and had now been at Tangley
two months.

Then Sybil wrote to Robert. She
begged him to come and see her once
again. There was in it, he fancied, an

underlying tone of reproach that he had
not been the one to yield to the desire of
meeting.

Her letter sent him to consult his usual
mentor, Mrs. Athelstane, whom he was
fortunate in catching on a day that she
had come to town.

" I tell it all to you," he said, "because
I believe you know it all already in
substance, if not in detail, and you know
her; and I want you to advise me as to
what I am to do now."

" But there is so little to advise," she
replied, when he had told her all. " There
is nothing to say. You must part; that
is all. I know how cruel it sounds; but
there are no two ways about it. It must
be done."

" Well," he persisted, " let me put before

you clearly how the case stands, and then tell me what I am to do. Here is a woman whom I love, and who, I believe, loves me. I believe I may say without presumption that I count for very much in her life, and there are few enough things in it that she can value. Here is a woman, then, whose present life is a misery, and whose future I believe I could make happy by taking her away out of her present. And—I may be doing her an injustice in saying it—but I believe she would be willing to come with me. What is my duty to that woman, putting my personal feeling out of the question—to leave her in misery or to take her to happiness ? "

Mrs. Athelstane was silent a few moments. Then she said, " Your duty

is to do your duty, and you know it; and
it cannot be your duty to run away with
another man's wife. You cannot be asking
the question seriously. Forgive me, too,
if I say that you are assuming too much.
You are assuming that her future with
you would be a perfectly happy one. In
such a future as you sketch there must
be drawbacks. But even putting that
aside (one need not go into the well-worn
casuistry of this question), your duty is
none the less clear."

"Yes, you are right; you are right. I
know you are right," said Robert sadly.

"My poor man, I am very sorry for
you," Mrs. Athelstane said; "but I know
you will do what is right in the end, however you are tempted. And what is right
in this case is, I am very, very sure, for

you to part from her definitely. Is it
not so ? "

" Yes, you are right," he admitted. " As
I say, I know you are right. But do you
know—despise me as you like, you cannot
despise me more than I do myself—I
cannot go to her, and say I will part from
her. I have not the hardness of heart—
no, I mean the strength of will—to
do it."

" Write it, then," Mrs. Athelstane said
remorselessly.

" Yes, I might write it," he said; "but
even that would not be final. It is not
altogether because I am a coward that I
do not go and tell it to her, gently and
firmly, before her face. I *am* a coward.
I do not think I could do it. I do not
believe any man could who loved. It is

well for women and novelists to picture
their hero as a being with a will like an
iron crowbar; but I can only say that I
never met any man at all like that yet.
It is the man's natural function to shield
the woman from cruelty, not to inflict it.
But apart from all this, as I say, it would
not be sufficiently final, were I to write
and speak as you suggest. I am so tied
here now by Parliamentary work and so
forth, that I cannot go away. I should be
sure to see her, and the whole wretched,
weak yielding and the misery would begin
again. I cannot see her so miserable, and
be hard with her. I cannot do it. I
repeat to myself—

> " ' I could not love thee, dear, so much,
>   Loved I not honour more,'

and all those little copy-book bits of

morality ; but they do not seem to strengthen me."

"But what do you wish me to say, then ? What did you come to me for, if you have come primed to meet every suggestion of honourable conduct by a simple confession of your weakness ?" She spoke in tones of scorn and surprise that he should think of acting so.

"Well, Mrs. Athelstane," he said, "if I had no suggestion to make upon my part, I should deserve everything bad that you could say of me. But I have something further to suggest ; something that I think of doing, and in which I wish for your advice. I have all but made up my mind to write to her, and tell her that I love her no longer ; at least, I could say that my love had changed into respect, affection, what you please ; but that it was no longer love. I could do that ; I could write anything, and that would, once for all, it seems to me, change her heart towards me. But I candidly confess to you—think of me what you will—in her hands, when I see her, I am as wax ; she can do anything with me. I can refuse her nothing in her misery that she asks of me."

"But it will be such an untruth," Mrs. Athelstane objected.

"Of course it will. It will, I admit," he said. "But there are circumstances, as it seems to me, which justify it. It is not the absolutely right thing to do, I know. A really good, strong man would go and say to her inflexibly, 'We must part ;' but I am not that good, strong man, and I literally cannot do it. The other I can do. Now, tell me, what do you think?"

She pondered for a minute in silence. "But doesn't she—isn't she strong enough to help you at all?" she asked.

Robert shook his head, without raising his eyes to her. She understood him to shrink from saying a word of the loving weakness of the woman he loved.

Again Mrs. Athelstane relapsed into thoughtful silence. Then she said, "I really do not know how I ought to advise you. I cannot think it would be right for you to write and tell her such an untruth as this, which would have the effect of uprooting the last thing in whose stead-fastness she trusts—her faith in you. No, whatever you do, I advise you not to do that. I cannot offer you any alternative advice; but I say do not do that. Dear me, what a mass of unhappiness there is in the world! I wonder why God has allowed me to be so happy."

"And is that all the advice you can give me?" Robert asked sadly.

"Yes," she said equally mournfully; "I believe it is. If I can think of anything, of course I will tell you."

CHAPTER XII.

HUSBAND AND WIFE.

ROBERT went back to his rooms in the Albany Courtyard, and sat down before a blank sheet of writing-paper, biting at his pen, in cruel perplexity.

"It is all very well for her to say 'don't do it,'" he kept repeating to himself; "but what else can be done? She had nothing to suggest. And how am I to say it? It seems an impossibility even to begin."

And then his surface thoughts wandered away among the street noises of Piccadilly,

(199)

while his whole, real self was absorbed in a profitless musing about this letter he had persuaded himself he ought to write to the woman he loved. At length he seemed to shake his ideas together, and commenced, with short preface, on the substance of his missive—

"I am beginning a letter of almost impossible difficulty. It is so very hard to tell just what I mean, and yet to guard against your misunderstanding me. It is to tell you, dear, that my love for you is not less, but altered. I seem to myself to be loving you not with less affection, but with less passion—more in the way in which you have so often said you wished we loved."

"Oh, what a liar I am!" he exclaimed, breaking off his writing, and throwing down his pen. But presently he goaded himself to take it up again, saying to himself, " Let me make an end of it."

" I cannot tell you," he wrote, "how this change has come about, or when. Probably it has been working, without my knowledge, for a long time, and it is only now that I seem to myself conscious of it. I do so hope that you will understand me in this. It is not that I love you less, but differently ; possibly with an even better love. I trust that we may love each other like brother and sister all the days of our lives."

He stopped, and read over what he had written.

" Oh, what a brute of a letter ! " he said, as he took it and tore it up, and with a savage satisfaction crumpled its fragments, and threw them into the waste-paper basket.

He walked about his room for half an hour or so, silently smoking. Then he sat down again, and penned another letter almost word for word identical with the former. He signed it, "Always yours, R. Burscough;" enclosed it in an envelope; addressed and stamped it, and put it in his pocket.

He carried it about with him all the afternoon. It was not that he forgot it. Far from that; he seemed to almost feel it hotly and constantly burning. He laughed with grim humour, as he thought to himself that it seemed to take twice the room in his pocket of an ordinary letter. The late session was not yet at an end, but it was Wednesday. The House

did not sit, and he walked about most of
the afternoon, avoiding his fellow-men.
When he came back to his rooms to dress
for dinner, the letter was still in his pocket.
He determined to post it at once, and
went out with that object. He would let
no one but himself post this particular
letter. As he turned out of the Courtyard
into Piccadilly, he nearly knocked down
a telegraph boy, who was rounding the
corner on the other tack.

"Beg pardon," Robert said, "who've
you got a telegram for? Burscough, by
chance?"

"Yes. Are you him?"

"Yes, I'm him," Robert said.

The boy gave a look, concluded it was
all right, and went off whistling selections
from "The Yoemen of the Guard."

Robert tore open the envelope. The message was short. "Do not come—Morningham."

He stood stock-still, gazing at the words.

"Hullo, Burscough, what's the matter?" asked a passing acquaintance. "Lost another bye-election?"

"No, no. The elections are all right," he answered, smiling vaguely.

His friend passed on, and Robert went slowly to his rooms.

"Thank Heaven!" he said, "that I ran into that telegraph boy. Two minutes later and I'd have posted that letter."

He took the letter out of his pocket and threw it into a desk, which he locked.

That very day, for good or evil, the fates had put it into Lord Morningham's

head to go to Tangley. He came quite
unannounced, and, leaving his bag at the
station, walked up to the cottage. He
rang the bell and told them to send for
the bag.

Sybil and her friend were upstairs in
the child's nursery, and heard the ring of
the bell.

" Who can it be ? " Helen exclaimed.

At the same moment Lord Morning-
ham's step in the hall sounded all over the
tiny house.

" Oh, Helen," said Sybil, "it's Morningham ! "

Helen's heart bled for her as she saw
how she turned pale and shivered, and
seemed to shrink into herself with fear
and loathing when she recognized her
husband's step.

He came upstairs and knocked at the door. "How do you do?" he said, as he came in.

"Oh, how d'you do? You have taken us quite by surprise. Excuse me a moment, I must see to baby."

She turned away; and Lord Morningham was left to make his greeting to Mrs. Athelstane.

"I thought I would come down to see how you were getting on," he said.

He addressed himself rather to Sybil, but as she did not answer, Mrs. Athelstane took upon herself to make some commonplace reply.

"Won't you come downstairs and have some tea?" Sybil presently asked. She spoke as if she were doing the honours of the house to a stranger.

" Thank you."

At tea he asked after their comfort and wants with ceremonious politeness, and to each inquiry Sybil answered in the same manner, that they wanted for nothing.

" Are you going to sleep here ? " she asked. " If so, I will give orders about your room."

" Yes ; only to-night," he said. " I must be off again to-morrow."

She went out as if to give the necessary directions, but after an interview with the housemaid, left the house, and going to the post-office, telegraphed briefly to Robert, " Do not come—Morningham."

That night, when she and Helen were together in the room which they shared, she knelt at her prayers long after her friend had finished and had got into bed.

When she rose from her knees, she went to Helen Athelstane, and laying her arm round Helen's neck, put her face down on the pillow beside the other's face. Helen felt that her cheek was all wet with tears.

"Oh, Helen, tell me," she whispered, "what am I to do? How am. I to bear it? Why does he come down here to torture me? I don't know how I am to go on bearing it. There is no use in praying; God will not hear me. How should He when I am so wicked—so wicked that I do not even seem to love my child?"

"Oh, hush, Sybil dear!" said Helen, whom this last self-accusation always shocked more than any other; "you mustn't talk like that."

Sybil did not answer. Soon she got quietly into bed, and lay for a full half hour without speaking. Helen hoped she was sleeping, but of a sudden she said—

" Helen, are you asleep ? "

" No," Helen answered.

" Well, listen then," she said in a tone which was full of resolve. " I have made up my mind that I will tell Morningham —that I will tell him that I love Robert Burscough, and that he loves me. Very likely he will kill me, but I don't think he will. It would be about the best thing that could happen to me perhaps, if he did. Of course, I shall tell him how honourably Robert has behaved, that he has parted from me because we felt we could not bear it ; and so, don't you see, it will make a barrier between me and Robert so that we cannot see each other—do you see ? "

" Oh, Sybil," said Helen, too much surprised to think out the consequences of the step, " that would be splendidly honourable of you ; but how do you think you will ever have the courage to do it ? "

" Yes, I mean to. I have made up my mind," Sybil said, as if the question were quite settled. " Good night, Helen dear, and go to sleep."

The next morning, as her husband was finding his train in the A. B. C., Sybil said to him, " Are you off directly ? Can you give me a minute or two ? "

" Yes, of course I can," he said, looking a little surprised. " If I start in half an hour or so it will do."

" I suppose," she said, speaking with

icy coldness, "that we are no longer supposed to keep up even to the outside
world the farce of pretending to love each
other."

"I—I do not know—I hadn't thought
about it," he stammered, taken aback by
the unexpectedness of the question.

She gave a short, bitter laugh. "Thank
you," she said; "that is a very candid
statement of your attitude towards me.
It is a point I wished understood. I
never flattered myself so much as to think
that my image filled your heart. Perhaps
the organ is too capacious. So that I was
not surprised when from time to time you
took to your heart images of several other
women to supply the place your wife ought
to have occupied."

Lord Morningham did not speak.

"Such being the case then," she went on in the same cold, even tone, "you will probably not be surprised to hear that I have taken to my heart, to supply the place which your image should have filled there, not quite so many loves as you have done—I have been content with one. It may interest you to hear," she said, with an insolence of defiance which her own words seemed to nourish, "that I love Robert Burscough, and that he does me the honour of returning it.

"Well?" Lord Morningham said in cold interrogation.

She said nothing.

"Is that all you have to say?"

"Yes."

"Ah! it was hardly worth making such a preamble over. I should have been quite

annoyed if it had made me miss my train.
Good-bye." And he went away.

Sybil sat still and silent.

She scarcely seemed to think. All feeling was numb in her. Mrs. Athelstane
came in and found her sitting so.

" Did you tell him ? " she asked.

" Yes," Sybil answered listlessly.

" And what did he say ? "

" Nothing ; and insulted me in saying
it. Really I do admire him sometimes."

" Don't, Sybil ; I hate you when you
are cynical. And you told him that you
had made up your minds to part. What
did he say to that ? "

" No, I forgot to tell him that."

" You did not tell him that. But you
must, Sybil. What will he think ? "

" I don't see that it much matters what he thinks."

And to all Helen could say to urge her to write and tell him, she replied but this—

" Oh no, it does not signify. I don't see that it matters what he thinks."

In the course of the afternoon she so far roused herself as to write these few words to Robert—

" I telegraphed to you not to come yesterday because he came down. I have told him that we love each other. Forgive me, but I could not help it. I did it in order to set an impassable barrier between us. Good-bye. Do not write to me. We must never see each other again."

A fortnight passed without incident or any change of her mood, but then her thoughts began to revert again very strongly to Robert Burscough. She tried to banish him from her mind, but his image would not be denied. It ever beset her. She fought against it with exasperated petulance, for, by some curious misapprehension, she had deemed that, once she had told her husband of the position of affairs between Robert and herself, it would be materially altered thereby. She was vexed to think that she had spoken in vain, that she had altogether missed her mark, and had made her position, if anything, less tolerable than before.

"You know, Helen," she said, "when I told Morningham, I thought it would somehow set up a barrier between Robert and me. It doesn't seem to have done it; it seems quite as possible for me to see him as it did before. Didn't it seem to you as if it would have set up a barrier?"

"Well, no," Helen answered. "I know you said it would, but I must say that even at the time I could not quite see how."

"Then why did you not tell me so?"

"Well, it seemed so altogether the right and honourable thing to do, Sybil, that though I should never have dreamt of suggesting it to you, yet when you said you were going to do it I would not say a word to turn you from it."

"Yes, I see," she said. "But it has not had a bit the effect I expected. I do not quite know why I should have thought it would. It only seems to have set up a greater barrier than ever between *him* and me. So far it is a good thing."

"Oh, Sybil!" said Helen reproachfully.

"Oh, but it is a good thing, a very good thing," she said bitterly. "I don't know how it is all to end, I'm sure," she went on wearily. "Sometimes I think I will just write straight to Robert Burscough, and ask him to take me away from it all. I suppose *he* would divorce me all right; and then I could marry Robert, and our lives might be all so different."

"Oh, don't talk like that," Helen pleaded. "Think of baby, Sybil."

"Oh no, don't tell me to think of baby," she said vehemently. "I tell you I believe I am grown quite devoid of natural affection."

"Oh, Sybil!" was again all Helen could say.

Sybil's tone suddenly changed. "No,

dear, you are right," she said, her mood suddenly softening. " I am a wicked, bad woman.   No, I will not write to Robert— never, if I can possibly help it."

CHAPTER XIII.

"THE WOMAN THAT DELIBERATES."

THE weather the last two days had changed. Before, it had been glorious : but now the sky was cloudy and lowering, and there were frequent showers. Sybil was still delicate, and was ordered to keep from the damp. They had to watch their opportunities to be out between the showers. Then came a day not showery, but of soaking, continuous downpour. Sybil had grown weary of reading. She felt as if she would not care if she never saw a book again. She never worked,

(219)

and the confinement of the house was very tedious to her. After tea, she stood for a long time drumming with her knuckles upon the window-pane, looking drearily out at the sodden trees and splashing rain.

"I'm going out, Helen," she said suddenly. "I don't care. I shall be stifled if I stay in here all day. It will not do me any harm if I keep walking all the time."

Helen did her best to dissuade her, but she would not be gainsaid. She put on an old tweed suit, and a boyish tweed hat, and, wrapping a handkerchief round her neck, started, with no umbrella, but with a crook handled walking stick, which she had brought from Scotland. Helen watched her walk briskly off along the path leading through the wood up on to the heath at the back. When she was out of sight, Helen went back with a sigh to her knitting.

In about an hour Sybil returned. Her face was aglow with the exercise ; her dress was darkened by the wet, and clung damply about her. Some locks, which had losened themselves from under her cap, hung heavy with the rain round her bright cheeks.

"Oh, it was glorious," she said. "I do love walking in the rain. There is a letter," pulling from her jacket pocket a pulpy, damp envelope. "I called at the post and found it."

Helen saw that the address was in Morningham's hand. She drew the letter from the envelope. But for the name outside—The Countess of Morningham—

there was nothing to show to whom it was written. "Do not hurry yourself to return," it said. "Perhaps you had better take on the cottage for a month or two longer.— MORNINGHAM."

"Oh, Sybil!" Mrs. Athelstane said indignantly. "What a shameful letter!"

"Of course, it's a shameful letter," said Sybil, with a forced cheerfulness that jarred on her friend. "What else did you expect it to be? There's much to be thankful for in it, though. I don't see what I could have expected better. I must go and change my things."

And she was out of the room before the other could answer.

But after dinner, in spite of her previous affectation of cheerful carelessness, she was moody and absorbed. For a while she pretended to read a book; then she got up suddenly and went to the writing-table. She dashed off these words—

"I can quite understand that you do not care to see me, but do you not care to see your child ?—SYBIL M."

She addressed it to her husband, sealed it, and, ringing the bell, ordered it to be taken at once to the post, though it could not go till the early mail next morning.

About noon the following day arrived the answer, by telegram—briefer even than any of the preceding missives—

" No.—MORNINGHAM."

She said nothing to Helen of either her letter or its answer. Once in the afternoon she came and laid her head upon Helen's shoulder. "Oh, Helen," she said ; " I think I shall go mad !" That was all.

For the most part her suffering was dumb. Nor was Mrs. Athelstane's sympathy expressed in words, but was none the less therefore understood. Most of Sybil's time, indeed, she now preferred to spend alone, wandering about among the pines, or over the heather-clad common beyond them. As a rule she did not ask Helen to accompany her, and Helen, by some tacit sympathy, comprehended her wish for solitude. Sybil seemed to have quite got over the nervous fear of being alone, which had once given her much suffering. Her actual sorrows were, perhaps, so engrossing as to leave no room for troubles of the imagination.

Nevertheless, she was far from well. She seemed possessed by a restless, feverish activity, and inability to sit still or occupy herself. Her clear complexion was pale, save for two patches of hot colour. It was as if some inward excitement were devouring her.

One morning, four or five days after the telegraphic "No," Mrs. Athelstane and Sybil were standing at the drawing-room window. Neither had spoken for several minutes, when suddenly Sybil turned, and, throwing her arms round the other's neck, said, with a burst of tears—

"Oh, I can't bear it any longer. I can't —I can't!"

Mrs. Athelstane sought to comfort her; but almost before she had said a word, Sybel recovered herself, and, drying her eyes, left the room. A few minutes later Mrs. Athelstane saw her leave the house. She was frightened at Sybil's words.

They suggested a meaning which she was afraid to admit, even to herself. She watched the path by which her friend went, then, running upstairs for her hat, hastened after her. When she came out Sybil was not in sight, but Helen hurried down the path which she had seen her take. Soon it bifurcated among the bushes.

Helen paused, uncertain which track to follow. Then she hurried up one which, so soon as she had rounded a corner of the bushes at some hundred or so yards, would, she knew, give her a long vista. When she came to the corner there was no one visible. A rabbit ambled lazily out of the path some fifty yards on. Clearly no one had been there. She hurried back and struck down the other path. It was more winding, and she could at no time see very far ahead; but at length it led clear of the trees. She climbed the stile on to the pathway across the open field. As she looked out over it, she exclaimed, "Oh!" her lips parted in horror, and she stood stock still.

Some three hundred yards or so from her—just across the field—a road led over the railway line by a bridge. Sybil was standing on the bridge, with her elbows resting on the parapet, peering over and down at the railway track below—with what thought in her brain? It was this that drew the exclamation from Helen Athelstane's lips, and froze her in horror to the spot where she stood.

For a moment she almost feared to call or to advance, in dread of hastening the tragedy she fancied imminent. Then she began to walk down over the field, at first slowly, then more quickly, until she finally broke into a run, and hurrying over the stile at the other fence of the field, was by her friend's side.

Sybil never knew of her approach until she felt her arms around her. Then she turned to her a startled face, as pale as death.

"What were you thinking of, Sybil?" the other asked in a hoarse whisper.

"Oh, Helen, dear, you'd better have let me do it," said she wearily, passing her hand over her forehead.

Then Helen took her home, and they had a long, long talk; and in the end Sybil made Helen a solemn promise never to think again of the dreadful deed which she had been contemplating against her own life.

They did not speak of it any more that day, and in the evening, Sybil, contrary to her habit, sat very still and thoughtful. When they went to bed Helen, in her anxiety for her friend, slept very little, and, so far as she could discover, Sybil did not sleep at all.

But the next morning she was brighter. She seemed composed, and less restless. Very soon after breakfast, Helen met her in the little hall with her hat on.

"It's all right, darling ; you may trust my promise," she said affectionately, in answer to a look which Helen had certainly not meant to be one of suspicion.

She went down to the village, where she took from her pocket a letter addressed to "Robert Burscough, Esq., M.P., Albany Court-yard, Piccadilly, London, W."

"When will a letter posted now be delivered in London?" she asked the girl.

The girl was a little indefinite, but thought some time early in the afternoon.

Sybil dropped her letter through the slit and went away. She did not go straight home, but into her favourite pine-wood. There she pulled from her pocket a scrap of paper, a copy of the letter to Robert, and, sitting on the elastic cushions of the pine needles, read it over. It was very short, like most of her letters :—

"Robert darling, come and take me away from this wretched life. I *cannot* bear it any longer. Yours, ever and only, SYBIL."

"It'll get there early in the afternoon," she said to herself; "perhaps about two. Then, if he should be in, he could catch the 3.20 train easily. I wonder if he will telegraph first. Or, perhaps he may not be in. No," she reflected sadly, "most probably he will not. He will be most likely lunching somewhere, and will just come in for a moment perhaps before four on his way to the House, and then he cannot get here till close on dinner time. But he is sure to telegraph in that case. Or possibly he may go straight to the House, and, if so, it all depend on what is going on at what time he will get it— perhaps not till he comes home to bed. If so, he would write at once, I should think, and I should get a letter by the first post. That is the most likely, after all. I will make up my mind not to expect to hear until to-morrow morning."

But though she said that she would make up her mind to expect nothing until the morrow morning, it was evident to her friend's sympathetic vision that she was all that day in expectation ; though of what, Helen did not know. She was on the alert for every sound and every step, but bed-time came, and there was no answer from Robert.

" He must have gone straight to the House," she said to herself. " I shall hear to-morrow morning."

But in the morning again there was no letter. There will be a telegram immediately, she thought. Mid-day came, and still there was no telegram. If she had been more composed the previous day, she had certainly on this morning a grave access of her fever. Most of the time she spent pacing up and down before the little house, jealously watching all the approaches, and striving to discern now the telegraph messenger in the baker's boy, now Robert's fly in the grocer's cart.

But no; she had to come in to luncheon, and there was still no news. Then she began to ask herself more connectedly what could be the reason of it. He might, indeed, be away, though that seemed most unlikely just now, when she knew him to be in the thickest of Parliamentary business at the close of the session. Still that was the only explanation—unless, indeed! But no, the very shadow of the thought made her hot—she could not entertain it. And yet, what a fearful thing it would be if this man, into whose arms she had so unreservedly thrown herself with her appeal, *ad misericordiam*, should reject her! Oh no ; he never could, after all that had passed between them.

And the afternoon wore away, and still no sign or message, until Sybil's thoughts and emotions wearied themselves of their own activity, into comparative apathy.

CHAPTER XIV.

A TERRIBLE MISTAKE.

ROBERT'S place as legislator had missed him that day. It was not that he was out of London; it was not that he was travelling down to Tangley; it was not even that he was writing to Sybil.

He had not been to his rooms at all on the previous day after breakfast time. On returning from the House about 12.30 in the morning, he had found Sybil's note lying on his table. That note consisted of about three lines. Therefore, when it is said that he spent by far the greater part

(235)

of what remained of the night in reading
it over and over, it might be thought that
by the morning he would have arrived at
some conclusion with regard to his action
concerning it.   But this was by no means
the case.   He made a pretence of breakfast, and then going to his desk, took out
the letter which he had written to Sybil
after his conference with Mrs. Athelstane,
and which, in consequence of his collision
with the telegraph boy, he had put into
his desk instead of into the post.   He did
not open the envelope of this letter, as he
had, indeed, no need to do, for he remembered word for word its contents ; but
kept turning it about in his fingers, like
a weak whist-player with the ace of trumps.

Eventually he threw it back into the
desk, which he locked, and, putting on a

"billy-cock" instead of the tall hat of conventional London, started for a long walk. He went up through Regent's Park and into the Zoological Gardens, whence, after envying the animals for a while, he went on towards Hampstead. He had bread and cheese at a hostelry of the name of the "Cock and Crown," and came back to London by way of Primrose Hill.

He had thoroughly tired his body ; but he had not made up his mind. It was about half-past four when he got back. The country post would soon be gone. What was he to do ? He once more took the familiar letter from his desk, and fingered it over again dubiously. Then he slowly put on his hat, and walked deliberately out and along Piccadilly. No opportune collision with a telegraph-boy on this occasion delayed him, though fancifully he almost expected it. He went on to Burlington House, and dropped his letter into the box, feeling as if he had dropped a missive for the Council of Three into the lion's mouth of mediæval Venice.

He dined alone, and went back to another night of little sleep, but of much question of what the answer would be— accusatory or supplicatory? The former he fervently hoped ; he doubted his own strength to bear the latter.

He reckoned that Sybil would receive his letter by the morning post, and that he might possibly have a reply early in the afternoon. He made heroic efforts to keep away from his rooms as long as possible, knowing that his impatience would be yet more intolerable if he came back to find no answer.

He returned about three, and found a letter in her handwriting along with two others. Disregarding these, he pounced upon Sybil's, and tore it open. It was in neither tone of his expectation. In length it was like most of her letters; in tenour, different.

" Kindly let me see you as soon as convenient, and let me have some explanation of your inhuman letter.

"S. M."

That was all. But one word—truly not lacking in significance—"inhuman," seemed to suggest the probable manner of her reception of him.

He telegraphed, " Will be down to-

morrow morning;" and went to the House
to endeavour to distract his mind with the
business of the nation.

On the morrow, in the train to Tangley,
he could not fail to draw a painful contrast
between the conditions of his last and those
of his present visit. In a vague way he
found himself wondering how Nature could
be so gaily beautiful and happy seeming,
while he was suffering such a load of
torture, both on his own account and for
the woman whom he loved and was forced
to make suffer.

There was no one to meet him at the
station. He walked up to the little house
by himself. The servant showed him into
the tiny drawing-room. No one was
there. In a few moments Sybil came in.
He was shocked by her pallor, and the

traces of suffering in the lines of her eyes and mouth. He made a movement towards her, but she passed by him with a slight bow, and without notice of the hand which he half offered her. She bowed to a chair, in which he obediently seated himself, while she remained standing, with one hand grasping the back of a chair behind her.

"Have you come to give me any explanation?" she asked, in a low but distinct and metallic voice.

He did not answer. What could he say?

"Do you not think I have a right to ask an explanation?" she continued—"I, whom you have told you loved better than the whole world, whom you have taught the meaning of the word love? Have I no right to ask you for an explanation, when you throw me off at the first moment that I offer myself to you—that I try you to see if there is any, the tiniest, bit of truth in one of the solemn asseverations you have made me ? Have I no right to ask for an explanation ?"

"Sybil dear," he said gently, taking no notice of a shudder which seemed to pass over her when he spoke her name; "I told you, not that I had ceased to love you, not that I loved you less (God knows that that is not true)," he went on, with a strange half sob, half laugh of despair at the truth which she would *not* believe, mingling with the cruel acting which she *would* believe. "It was only that I loved you differently, that the nature of my love seemed changed." "Oh," he murmured

to himself, as, with a groan, he buried his
face in his hands, " I cannot do it! I
cannot speak. If I speak at all, I cannot
do it."

She looked at him strangely for a
moment, a transient tenderness crossing
the anger of her eyes. Then she said—

" We can fully understand each other,
I hope. Will you, please, tell me this
plainly: if I were a free woman now,
would it be the first wish of your life to
make me your wife ?"

"Sybil," he answered, " I told you, did
I not ? I told you that my love had
altered, that—— "

" Thank you," she said ; " that is quite
enough. That is all that I wished to
know. Oh, you need not remind me
of what you told me. The words of

your letter are burnt into my brain. I can never forget them. My very brain seems as if it were on fire. But, of course, that is all of no consequence to you. Will you understand this, then, please—that I reject your offer of brotherly affection? It is an insult to me. I do not love you as a brother, and I cannot pretend to. I pray God that He may teach me to loathe you. But remember this—perhaps it may be very flattering to your vanity to hear it —that here in me you have one blasted life and broken heart to answer for. My life was anything but happy, it is true; but, still, I might perhaps have borne it, had you not come back into it and re-minded me what it was to love. It has been only child's play to you—a passing amusement; but to me it has been a cruel

shattering of all my faith, my hope, my
life. Yes, you ; actually you, whose amusement it is to go about making second-class
love to married women—I had actually
raised you up as an idol in my heart. I
trusted you, I tell you, as I would have
trusted my God ; and now—good heavens !
What a poor fool I was ! How you must
have laughed at me the while ! Perhaps
my first lesson should have taught me
better ; but my husband, at least, never
pretended that he loved me."

And he sat there in silence, in silence
that seemed utterly shamefaced, and heard
himself accused of all imaginable baseness
and untruth, without saying a word in his
defence. He did not murmur at his
punishment, at the remorseless words with
which she scourged him, for was not his

executioner the woman whom he loved, and for whose very sake he bore the shameful stripes which she laid upon him ?

" Have you nothing to say to me ? " she asked.

" No," he said sadly, shaking his head, " no ; nothing."

" Then go. Please go," she pleaded, in a faint voice, almost choked by a sob. " Stop, though ! stop a minute ! " she exclaimed, recovering herself with the necessity for action, and, going to a drawer, took out a photograph of Robert. " Take this with you," she said ; " it seems to haunt me, for, put it where I will, in any desk or drawer, your false, cruel, wicked face seems to look up at me, and pierce through everything."

She thrust the photograph vehemently

into his hand, and, sinking down upon a sofa, buried her face in her handkerchief, and made great efforts to restrain her weeping. He hesitated a minute, and turned with his hand on the door knob. He looked at her irresolutely. Then, with an inarticulate groan, he went from the room and from the house.

The next day Sybil did not come down to breakfast. She had slept hardly at all, and looked most wretched. She had intended to get up later; but when the maid came, she sent her away with impatient fretfulness. She stayed in bed all day, telling Helen that she was not ill, but had a headache. The next day she was no better. Helen insisted upon sending for the nearest country doctor. She would have wished to have sent for the Morning-

hams' doctor from London ; but Sybil was
peremptory on this point, that she would
see no one from London.   There was
nothing the matter with her, she declared.
In this she was supported by the country
doctor, who suavely prescribed freedom
from worry, perfect physical and mental
quiet.   He also wrote a prescription for
some stuff, which Helen had made up, but
which Sybil did not take.   Instead, she
took some chloral, which gave her a few
hours' much-needed sleep, and on the
fourth morning she roused herself, came
down to breakfast, and resumed her normal
ways.

But there was a difference in her—a
difference which her friend dreaded to
observe.   She had been unhappy before,
but it was unhappiness which had variable

moods. At times she had been almost light-hearted; at others, sunk in often tearful despondency. But now she had but one mood—melancholy. Before, Helen had deemed it good for her that she should go off and wander by herself among the pine trees or upon the heath, and seek what soothing influences kind Nature would send her. But now she feared to see her go forth alone, and would after a time start in search of her, so uneasy did she feel if Sybil were long absent. At meal times or in the evening in the house she would sit silent and uninterested, some-times pretending to read, but never turning a page, buried in such apathy that it was hardly even thought. She used to go out with a pencil and sketch-book, but it seemed as if, on coming home, she never

had any result to show for these prepara-
tions.   She took but the most perfunctory
notice of her child, and was as one perfectly indifferent to her surroundings.

" If only she could have some change—
something to rouse her!" Helen said to
herself sadly, not seeing how by any means
such a change was to be brought into her
life.

One day Helen went out to seek her in
the pine wood, where she spent so many
of the hours.   At first she could   see
nothing of her, and at length, affected by
the mystery of the place, leant against a
great pine bole and became lost in reverie.
When she lifted her eyes, she saw Sybil
coming towards her.   She was walking
along the pathway which led close beside
the tree by which Helen stood.   The

elder woman watched the younger, who had known so many more years of sad experience, with a sense that there was a suggestion of unearthliness about her. For she was walking with wrapt, upturned eyes, as if expecting a vision.

" Is it not wonderful, Helen ?" she said, coming to her without question of why she were there, as if it were the most natural thing in the world to see her standing idle against the bole of any pine tree in the wood. " Is it not wonderful ? I often look down the dark vistas of these columns almost in the expectation of seeing some one or other of the gods walking towards me betwixt them ; but I think that there is but one god or goddess, namely Death, and that some day I shall see her coming to me, white-robed, between the columns, and that then I shall know Death's truth."

" Sybil, Sybil darling!" said her friend, taking her hand, "how strangely you talk. You must not talk like that."

She laughed. "Oh, I am all right, dear. You need not be afraid for me. I shall not go off my head now. I thought I might have done so once, but there is no such luck in store for me now. It is Hope that is the bondsman, you know. Despair is free. What says he?

> ' You are a slave, my dear,
>   Bound hard with a heavy chain,
>   Forged of a thousand subtle links
>   Of doubt, and fear, and pain.
>
> ' Free as the wind am I,
>   Free as the birds of the air,
>   My liberty knows no limit,
>   My freedom is called Despair.' "

"Yes," she repeated, with a mocking laugh—

> "'*My* liberty knows no limit,
> *My* freedom is called Despair.'"

"My poor Sybil!" said Helen, passing her arm round her friend's waist. And in this loving, schoolgirl fashion, they went back together to the house.

"Oh," Sybil exclaimed, "I should love to be able to give human voice to the voices of the wind and the forest. Listen," she said, as she produced a leaf torn from her sketch book. "I have tried to do it; it is the storm. How roughly he woos the trees!

> 'Soft o'er the billowing grass he stole on a slumbering forest,
> Rushed on her shivering leaves—rent at her clustering tresses—
> Soon in her heart of hearts, in swelling and deepening bass-notes,

Lifted his voice and roared, confounding and deaf'ning
　　her senses
To cries of her tortured limbs in strange embraces
　　complaining,
Or deeper groan of her pain, or myriad snapping of
　　branchlets,
Or crackle and rending crash of great main member
　　splintered ;
Hushed down, and hushed him away—woke with a
　　threatening shudder—
Sank again restfully down—left her a moment of
　　respite—
Surged up again thro' her leaves, in ever gathering
　　tempest,
Swelled and roared in his rage, till the roots of the
　　forest were troubled ;
Sank him again to his rest—and grumbled, aloof, as
　　he watched her—
Sighed away over her trees and left her alone in her
　　ruin.'"

" Why, it's splendid, Sybil," said Helen.
" Do you mean to say you wrote all that ?
It's wonderful—its poetry."

Sybil laughed gently. " Oh no, it isn't,
Helen. That's just what it isn't ; it isn't

poetry. There may be some feeling, some little imagination even, in it, perhaps, but there is no art. It is all confused."

"Well, it seems to me wonderful," Helen repeated.

"So it is very wonderful. A wood is always very wonderful to me. There is the sighing roof of the pine trees overhead and the softest cushioned carpet underfoot, and among the great pine stems one seems to be in some many columned temple of the gods. Wonderful! I should think it is wonderful."

Helen was greatly comforted by this little revelation. She had not her friend's deep love of Nature, but none the less rejoiced that Sybil should be able to find this companionship and distraction.

CHAPTER XV.

ALL this while they had seen nothing of Morningham. Neither had Robert seen anything of him, but had heard rather too much. This modern Babylon of ours is not a prudish city. It does not greatly concern itself with the morals of its citizens, even if they be caught red-handed in social crime. But what it does insist upon is this, that if caught you must at least show a pretence of shame. However thin the veil, you must decently play the hypocrite behind it. If you do not so,

(256)

you show a contempt of court—of the mighty bar of social opinion, which is infinitely more criminal than the crime for which you are summoned to it. And it was thus that Lord Morningham was offending. His own house even became the notorious scene of what society papers of the lower and more carrion-feeding class referred to darkly as "orgies." And this, society will not endure. The Englishman's house is his castle, and not only so, but, whatever his behaviour outside that castle, society requires that it shall be externally a whited one.

Robert was in deep distress. The matter became subject of common club gossip. "Lady Morningham should get a divorce," all said. His heart leapt within him at the suggestion of a divorce which should set free the woman he loved, yet he shrank from the thought of the trying publicity and distress which it must bring upon her. Moreover, was she at all likely to move in the matter? She, buried away there in the country, had probably heard nothing of her husband's mode of life. Was it not his own duty then?—no, not his, for had he not utterly cut himself off from her?—but the duty of her father or of some friend to open her eyes, and persuade her to take the steps required by the duty she owed to herself?

Yet, with a sensitive delicacy, he shrank from setting to work, even in the most indirect manner, any such machinery, lest a motive not entirely free of self-seeking might possibly lurk therein.

Meanwhile, Sybil and Helen had been

living their quiet life at Tangley, apparently under precisely the same conditions as before. Yet there had been a change. For, one day, as Sybil came in from her pine wood, something—the atmosphere she brought in with her, a difference in her step—made Helen look up with quick inquiry. And there was something new in Sybil's face to answer her. Something; but what? It was a light in her eyes, an uplifting of the weight off her brows—in a word, it was peace.

"What is it, dear?" Helen said, rising to meet her.

"I have found it, Helen. It has come to me; I knew it must. But it has come to me in a different way from anything I had expected. I was wicked. I said I should see Death's truth—that there was no god but Death ; but now I know that there is truth in life, that God, if He pleases, will give us His truth, will give us a communion with Him, even in this life. That is what has come to me to-day, Helen darling—the knowledge of a possibility of a communion with God such as I have never had, not only all through these years of wickedness, but in all my innocent, happy life which went before. Where is baby ? I must go and see her."

Puzzled, Helen Athelstane did not at all know what to make of it. Her nature, which had never been through so fiery an ordeal as her friend's, was not touched by the like mental and emotional crises. She had often and often, in these days at Tangley, feared for that friend's reason, and she had suspicions even of the present blessed phase just announced. But as the days wore on, and it became evident that whatever vision or visitation it were that had met Sybil in the "many columned temple of the pine wood," it was a visitation which had brought her a peace that did not seem likely to fail, then Helen began to admit to herself a hope that the worst days of warfare, of warfare between the elements of her own nature, might be over for her friend.

For, curiously enough, though it was there that she had found her happiness, Sybil now spent less time among the pine-trees. She had a new-found love for her baby, a new-found love for all around her, was able to find her own interests in whatseoever might be the interests of those about her.

The days went by tranquilly, and seldom did a whisper from the world reach them, when one afternoon, quite unannounced, as they sat at five o'clock tea, a fly drove to the door, and from it stepped out Mr. Davies.

He greeted them in his queer cynical way, and laughingly said he had come to spy upon them in their hiding-place; but both knew that there was something behind this, and Helen slipped away, leaving Sybil and her father together.

Then the father, with great gentleness, began to explain the object of his visit. Curbing his disposition to jest on the most serious and painful subjects, he told her, as tenderly as he could, of Morningham's doings, saying that they had now become a public scandal. Sybil listened to him

with growing disgust, but with a calmness
at which he marvelled. He then said that
he had come to consult with her on the
proper steps.

"Can it not all be let alone?" she
asked, greatly to his surprise. "I do not
think he will bother me any more."

"It certainly cannot be allowed to go
on as it is," her father said decidedly. "It
is an indignity to yourself and all connected with you."

"Do you mean to say that there will
have to be proceedings for divorce, that
our names will have to be dragged through
the mire?" she said in horror. "Think
what it will be to my child when she
grows up. I could not endure that.
Besides," she added, "I suppose he has not
been what they would call 'cruel' to me."

"I think there is no doubt you could get a divorce if you wished," he said; "but at least some arrangement must be made by which it shall be impossible for him ever again to claim, without your consent, a husband's rights, and also to secure to you the custody of your child. My poor girl, how you must have suffered! I fear I have been greatly to blame about you, my Sybil. If your mother had lived, things would have been very different for you."

"No, no, father," she said; "you have always been all that was kind;" and then she threw herself into her father's arms, and told him all the outlines of the sad story of her life, and at the end of her recital, her own eyes were certainly the drier of the two.

But on one point she was very determined. There should be no action for
divorce. For her child's sake she was
resolved that this should be so, and Mr.
Davies went back to London to arrange
with Lord Morningham's lawyers a scheme
for separation.

CHAPTER XVI.

THE NEMESIS OF WEAKNESS.

MRS. ATHELSTANE took the first opportunity of telling Robert the resolution which Sybil had taken with regard to her future. When she had finished, he was a long while silent.

"Is that what you would wish for her?" she asked, "that she should be compelled to live out her life alone?"

"Oh no, indeed it is not," he faltered.

"I was surprised," she said, "when her father told me her decision. I cannot think but that she will repent. Do you

(266)

not think that you might have some
influence in making her reconsider it ? "

" No, no," he said. " I could not go to
her now. I have made her loathe me.
She would not see me now unless all were
explained."

" Unless all were explained ! All
what ? " Mrs. Athelstane asked.

" About my writing to her as I did."

" Your writing to her ! that letter you
spoke to me about ? But I thought
you had not sent it—that you got a
telegram——"

" I did, yes. The first time I got a
telegram. But she wrote to me again and
asked me to—to see her, and I—I sent it
then."

" What, that dreadful letter telling her
you had ceased to care for her ? "

He nodded sorrowfully.

"Oh, you should not have done that. Why did you do that ?"

" Because I saw no other way for it. I had not the strength for the other way," he said wretchedly.

" And she still thinks of you like that ?"

"Yes," he said.

"Well, then, as you say, it must all be explained. You made a terrible mistake in sending that letter. But it must be explained. As soon as I get down to Tangley, I will tell her and do my best for you."

It was settled between them that Robert should hold himself disengaged to come to Tangley on receipt of a telegram.

" I think I shall be able to make her believe in the truth of what I shall tell her; but I cannot be certain. It will be very hard for her."

All the afternoon and the following morning, Robert was in his rooms in a state of impatience bordering upon madness. It was possible that the telegam should come at any minute, and he was determined that it should find him ready.

He sat with his hat and stick on a chair beside him, reading again and again in the A B C the times of departure and arrival for Tangley. But the hours passed, and still there was no telegram. His luncheon was brought in, and taken away untasted. But at four o'clock his door was opened by the servant, bearing a telegram on a silver waiter.

He almost dashed at the waiter, seized the telegram, and tore it open.

" Be at my house at five. Do not hope too much.—H. ATHELSTANE."

He crumpled the missive in his hand, threw it on the ground, and went and looked vaguely out of window. One might have supposed him absorbed in watching the traffic of Piccadilly.

What could it mean ? "Do not hope too much." Did it mean that all hope was over ? He picked up the crumpled telegram, smoothed it out, and read it again. But its sense was not altered. He looked at his watch—a quarter past four. He could walk across the Green Park to Mrs. Athelstane's house. By that time it would be nearly five. On his way thither he found occasion to notice that his surface attention was morbidly alive to the most trivial things—the twittering, cheeky

London sparrows, the very stones on his path—while all the time this fever of anxiety was throbbing in his brain.

Mrs. Athelstane came in immediately after he had been shown into the drawing-room.

" Poor man," she said ; " how ill you look ! "

" Oh, tell me," he said hungrily. " What did she say ? Did she not believe ? "

" Yes—yes ; she believed you," Mrs. Athelstane said. " Yes. She told me to tell you that—that she believed you, and that she thanked God that it had been proved to her that you, in whom she had had such trust, had not been false ; but that you had done it all for what you believed to be her good. ' But tell him, too,' she said, ' that I can never marry him now.' And when I pressed her for her reasons, she would say no more than that she would never marry, and that for the sake of her child she would not have a divorce.

"I think that Sybil has changed some-how. I do not know what it is, but she seems different—there is something almost unearthly about her—no, no, I don't mean that," Mrs. Athelstane added quickly, seeing a look of horror come over Robert's face, as if he understood her to mean that Sybil's mind was affected. "It is not that. I never saw her or any one more calm and collected ; but there is a change, though I cannot tell where it is."

"Do you think I might go and see her ?" he asked, in a broken voice.

"Yes, certainly ; indeed she told me to

say that she hoped you would.   I should like you to go and see her, for I think then you would understand better how it is.   I feel that I cannot explain it to you properly."

He took his leave very sadly, but a little inspirited by the thought of his visit to Tangley on the morrow, whither Mrs. Athelstane was returning the same evening. Accident or fate had woven very closely into the most notable features of his life this little house among the Surrey hills. He walked from the station to the cottage. When he came within sight of it, Sybil and Helen and the baby were at the door.   Sybil turned as she heard his feet on the gravel.   She gave a little start as she saw him.   Then she came out quickly.

"Oh, Robert," she whispered, as she gave him an earnest handshake. "I thank Heaven that it has been shown me that you were a true man. Have you really been able to forgive me all the dreadful things I said to you?"

There was no time for him to answer except by a responsive pressure of the hand, for they now met Helen Athelstane, with the child in her arms. But soon Sybil took him into the little drawing-room, while her friend stayed with the child out of doors.

"Tell me," Robert said quickly, as soon as they were alone. "Mrs. Athelstane gave me all your messages—*all.* Did you really mean them all?"

"Yes, dear, I did," she said, in a sad, sweet voice, not affecting to misunderstand him. "I meant what I said; I shall never marry now."

"But, Sybil, think of it," he said impetuously; "I can understand that you must shrink from the publicity of the divorce, and so forth——"

But she interrupted him. "No, it is not that," she said, still in the same gentle voice. "It is true that I am glad to think, for my child's sake, that there need be no legal divorce; but, Robert, forgive me,"— laying a gentle hand on his arm—"if I were a free woman this moment, I could not marry you now. I do not know why it is—I can't explain myself—but from the very moment that I got that letter from you which made me believe you cruel, false, and everything that was bad—you, on whom I had trusted more than in

anything in the world or above it—from
that moment my love became dead.   It is
not a thing that can be commanded, this
strange thing, love; and though I now
know, thank God, that in all the torture
to which you put me, you were acting for
what you believed to be the best (and I
thank you earnestly for it, and beg you
to forgive, if you possibly can, all I then
said to you—I can never hate myself
enough for those cruel words—I grow hot
with shame as I think of them), still,
though I can summon back all my old
affection and respect and faith in you yet,
the love does not come back.   Forgive
me, dear, if I hurt you (it has been our
fate to make each other suffer very
bitterly); but I should be doing you a
far greater hurt and wrong if I did not tell

you how my heart feels at this moment. I can never love you now. The act to which my own wrong-headedness drove you has killed the capacity in me. You have had the whole love of my life; and love has passed and gone out of it. You were once my only support, and perhaps it was God's will that that support should be 'taken from me in my worst hour of need, in order to prepare the way for the support which I have learnt to find in Him."

"Well?" Mrs. Athelstane said anxiously, as Robert came out of the house half an hour later.

He shook his head sadly. "No, it is not well."

"Her decision is quite unalterable, then?" (But she had already learnt the truth from his face).

"Yes; quite."

"And is she not in some way changed ? What do you think it is ? "

"I do not know," he said ; "but I think it is that in some mysterious manner she has found her way to God."

"Well, remember," she said, "do not give up hope; a woman's mind is not like the laws of the Medes and Persians."

He hurried off towards the station before she could say more to comfort him, and within an hour the train had brought him to the London terminus. As he hurried through the station wrapped in reverie, he came in direct collision with an elderly gentleman, who exclaimed, in courteous confusion—

"Pardon me, pray, my dear sir, my unfortunate shortness of vision."

Robert, in the midst of all his grief, could not but laugh. It was Mr. Fleg. When their mutual apologies were made, and Mr. Fleg's spectacles fairly resettled in their place, the latter said—

"And whither are you going, my dear sir?"

"I'm going several whithers," Robert answered. "First, I'm going to catch another man on the other side of the House, and pair off for the rest of the session. Then I'm going down to Little Pipkin (I shall telegraph to you which day I am going, and you'll come over and stay with uncle and me—for ever, most likely), and there I am going to paint a big picture. I'm probably going to give up politics; they bore me. Are there any more 'whithers' you want to know about?"

He spoke lightly; but Mr. Fleg detected trouble. The double glasses beamed with such searching scrutiny that Robert shied out of their line.

"Good-bye," he said; "good-bye."

"Pray stop one moment, my dear sir. I have a piece of interesting intelligence to impart to you. Our good young American friend, Mr. Cheadle, the younger, is engaged to be married."

"To be married, no! To whom? How 'the Braes o' Mar' will be going!"

"Miss Elsie Dormer, my dear sir; she whom we used to call 'the blind girl.' I have but just received a cablegram."

"And have you cabled congratulations?"

"I was this moment upon the point of so doing, my dear sir," the Professor replied.

"Come along, then; we'll do it together;" and, linking his arm in his old
friend's, Robert walked him off.

They cabled young Cheadle and Miss
Dormer messages which ran into several
pounds' cost, and left the clerk with no
doubtful opinion of their sanity. Then at
length they parted. Mr. Fleg stood looking after Robert's vanishing figure in the
absent-minded way which made him a
source of steady income to pickpockets.

" It's a pity," he said aloud, apparently
addressing himself to the sandwich man
who was standing on the kerbstone in all
the dejection of occasional sobriety—" a
great pity! A good young man, and of
great gifts, but a creature of circumstances
all his life through. Maybe we all are,
but it is disappointing. I had better
hopes. And he had every chance. The

story of his life might make a novel—a novel without a hero."

But the "creature of circumstances" carried out his present purposes and arrived at his "whithers," as explained to Mr. Fleg; for he paired off for the rest of the session. He also came down and lived at Little Pipkin with Professor Fleg and the Colonel; for the latter, having recovered his eight thousand pounds, which now seemed a far larger sum than before it was in such peril, had no scruple in accepting his nephew's bounty, since it was no longer necessary to him—such is the way of Colonel Burscoughs and the like.

It was then that Robert painted a picture which was never exhibited, of Slocombe in his cottage parlour—a picture which has more genius, as it has more faults, than any of those later ones by which he is known to fame.   For it is an adequate expression of a man who was not altogether a creature of circumstances, because in his infinite charity he can still say, " Nobody never has done me wrong"—and the truth of this statement, as of all others of Mr. Slocombe, receives the constant endorsement of the " Quack, quack!" of the old white drake.

THE END.

PRINTED BY WILLIAM CLOWES AND SONS, LIMITED,
LONDON AND BECCLES.;